DEATH IS LONG OVERDUE

AMY E. LILLY

BELLA LILLY PRESS
SPANISHBURG, WV

Cover Art by Ashley Townsend
ISBN-13: 978-0-692-41018-9

DEDICATION

FOR LILY, NATALIE AND GABRIELLA

CHAPTER ONE

"Know what your problem is?" Juliet threw popcorn into the air, tried to catch it with her tongue and missed.

"No," I sighed and bent to pick up the errant kernel. My sister is a slob. "But I bet you're dying to give me profound words of wisdom from your twenty-five years on the mountain, oh great guru."

"Your problem is that you're too nice, Phee. You need to stand up to people or you will be a doormat for the rest of your life," Juliet declared. She stretched her long legs out and rested her feet on my antique cherry coffee table. She wiggled her hot pink toes at me. I sighed and nudged them off with my own short hobbit-like feet. I loved my baby sister, but she would never understand. She was tall and blonde and could roll out of bed looking like a Paris fashion model. If I rolled out of bed, my short curves would keep on rolling and I would end up looking like a bag lady in a back alley. She was artsy, and I was just, well, kind of old-fartsy.

"I am not too nice!" I protested. "Today I left a very nasty message on Huey Long's answering machine. I told him that if he didn't bring the library's books back I would turn him into collections and ban him from the building. Would you believe he had the nerve to pinch me on my butt? I would've kicked him, but Charlie Cochran told him to get out before he knocked him out. Huey ran off as fast as his little legs could carry him. He should be terrified I will kick him in the place where it counts! I've had about all I can take of him. He's been skulking around the library for the past few months asking me out. He asked if he could 'check me out, take me home and read me.' The man is such a pig!" I pretended to gag. As the librarian at the small local library, I knew almost everyone in town. Sometimes it was hard to be mean to someone you might sit next to at the counter of Odd Couple's Diner. For Huey Long, I could make an exception.

"Whoa! You are B.A. I'm sure he was trembling in his little itty bitty troll boots he made from the hides of baby kittens. Did he bring back the books?" Juliet asked.

"B.A.? What the heck is that?" I wrinkled my nose in confusion. I found a few more dropped kernels of popcorn and leaned over to pick them up.

"Bad ass. You're such a nerd! Listen, Phee. Tell that little pervert the next time he touches you, you will drop kick him so hard that they'll find him in the next town. Threaten to charge him with assault, too. He is such a creeper. It would do him good to spend a night in jail." Juliet stood up, slipped on her shoes and grabbed her jacket and purse. "I love you just the way you are, but you need to try living a little more dangerously and be more assertive towards people. I'm saying this for your own good. Try new things. Realize there's more to the world than Miller's Cove, your books and your library. For heaven's sake, go on a date!

I bet I know a smoking hot deputy you wouldn't kick out of bed if given half the chance." She winked at me. I ignored her

"Huey Long is not a troll. He is a vertically challenged pervert," I snickered. I followed Juliet as she made her way to the door.

"Funny. Don't forget dad's birthday is a week away. Mom is in full party planning dictator mode so make yourself scarce," Juliet warned me as I shut the front door behind her.

I leaned my forehead against the wall and considered banging my head against it in frustration. Crud! How could I forget Mom's big party for my dad's sixtieth birthday? I would need to go shopping.

In the meantime, I thought about what Juliet said about standing up for myself. Too nice. Ha! I would show her. I would get the books back from Huey if it killed me. Now I just needed to figure out how to do it without actually dealing with him. Time to put all those hours logged reading crime novels to good use.

CHAPTER TWO

At nine o'clock, I put my book retrieval plan into action. I had spent the afternoon and evening preparing. Black shirt. Check. Black yoga pants with black riding boots. Check. Black ski mask bedazzled with a large "L" in the middle of the forehead. Check.

I donned my disguise and instantly transformed into Super Librarian who retrieves overdue library books with a single shush. I stuffed a small penlight into my red bra, grabbed my bag and headed out on Operation Book Snatcher.

I drove my beloved 1968 light aqua blue and white VW van, Velma, to Huey's house on Oakwyn Street. It was safe to assume he wouldn't be home because it was karaoke night at Carbuncle's Cabana on the Cove. He was known for his bleating renditions of Willie Nelson's *Sunny Side of the Street*. Karaoke started at eight o'clock, and Huey liked to be the opening act. Perhaps he thought it might increase his chance of getting lucky. I thought his chances might increase if he waited until the regular barflies downed a few drinks. Huey might look better after five shots of tequila. Okay, ten shots.

I parked Velma and strolled down the street towards Huey's house. I carried a leash in my hand so if I ran into anyone I could pretend to be looking for my dog. I prayed my Maine Coon cat, Ferdinand, would never find out about my betrayal of his species. I walked through Mrs. Grimes' dark back yard. Bless her for being too cheap to turn on her outside lights. Katherine Grimes was as deaf as she was blind. I was confident my outfit and bedazzled mask camouflaged my mad dash across her yard. I made my way into Huey's yard through his side gate. Tiptoeing through his tulip beds, I peered around and spotted a window that was open just a crack. I slowly pushed it up and cringed when it squeaked.

Not daring to open it further, I hoisted myself up and pulled myself through the gap. Suddenly, I stopped. I was stuck. My butt would not fit through the window. My love of dark chocolate cursed me. I wiggled and shimmied until I felt myself slide. Then I slid right out of my pants and onto the floor with a loud *thunk*. I jumped up and tugged up my pants. I held my breath while I waited for the sirens. My rear hitting the floor probably caused a small earthquake felt in three counties.

After a few terrifying moments, I heaved a sigh of relief and switched on my small penlight. I looked around the room. I spied a desk with an open laptop, a large sectional couch and in front of it, a coffee table stacked with books. My overdue library books. I started across the room.

As I neared the table, I felt my foot catch on something on the floor. Quickly righting myself before I fell, I shone my light downwards. Huey wasn't at karaoke tonight. I didn't think he would get lucky with the ladies ever again. I had tripped over one very naked, very erect and very dead midget.

CHAPTER THREE

"Come on, come on. Pick up!" I hissed into my cell phone as I hit redial and called Juliet for the fifth time. She finally answered.

"Could the timing be any worse? When I didn't answer the phone the first four times you called, it was a hint that I might be busy. You know what I mean?" Juliet giggled. I heard music and a man's muffled voice in the background.

"I'm in big trouble! Stop whatever you're doing because I need you to meet me right now! I don't have time to explain on the phone. Meet me on Oakwyn Street. Velma is parked across from Longfellow Park. Be there in 15 minutes!" I whispered and hung up. I shined the light across the room again. It lit on Huey's body, and I saw something tied around his neck. Fear knotted my insides as I realized he might be dead from something other than natural causes. I had broken into his house dressed all in black with a bedazzled mask. Great. I needed to get out of the house and fast. I grabbed the library books and took one final glance at the body on the floor. Not wanting to risk the window again as my escape route, I inched my way down the hall until I found the kitchen. The door was slightly ajar. I left the house as fast as my short legs could carry me and ran towards Velma not caring who saw me.

Twenty minutes later, Juliet's Karmann Ghia convertible pulled up behind me. A moment later, she opened the door and slid into the passenger seat. She looked at me and gave a loud snort. "What the heck is on your forehead? Is that an L?" Her grin grew wider. "And why is it on a mask? Taken up bank robbery as a night job? Hey if you need a few bucks..."

"Be serious. This is no time to be funny, Juliet!" I snapped. "This whole ordeal is your fault. You said quit being so nice and go live a little. I took your advice and decided to get all those books back from Huey. I created my very own superhero, Super Librarian, to execute Operation Book Snatcher. And that, my dear little sister, is what the "L" stands for."

"Um…Phee, I hate to tell you this, but an "L" in the middle of your forehead is what the cool kids say stands for loser." She made an "L" with her thumb and forefinger and put it to her forehead. "I hope you didn't drag me away from the most magnificent date ever so I could give you fashion advice. Super Librarian? Operation Book Snatcher? Have you switched from mysteries to comic books? Let me guess. There is an evil super genius with eight arms lurking in the bushes, and you need my help to defeat him."

"Huey Long is dead." As the enormity of what I found in the house hit me, I collapsed back against my seat and burst into tears.

"Holy crap! You killed him over some freakin' overdue books! What the..." Juliet looked at me in horror.

"I didn't kill him!" I sobbed. "I went into his house to get the books back when he was supposed to be at karaoke. I found him dead on the floor." Juliet reached into my glove compartment for some napkins. I took them and blew my nose.

"Whew! That's a relief. Just a little felony breaking and entering. Not murder. Glad you cleared that up," Juliet said with only a hint of sarcasm. "So what? You found him dead. Poor little troll. His heart probably gave out from reaching up to pinch too many women's asses. I assume he had a heart attack. We'll call 911 and say we came to see Huey. When he didn't answer the door, we walked in and discovered his body."

"I don't think that he just dropped dead all of a sudden. In fact, I know he didn't. There was something wrong with him. I can guarantee that somebody murdered him and now the cops are going to think it was me!" I cried harder.

"What do you mean? Wrong? Tell me what you saw," Juliet demanded.

"I was walking across the living room to grab the books when I stepped on him. I looked down and there he was. Naked with his eyes staring up at me and his tongue hanging out and his..." I stopped.

"His what? So far I don't see how this is a murder. It sounds like he was walking around in his birthday suit and dropped dead," Juliet said. "Dead doesn't mean murdered, Phee. Come back to reality and out of your mysteries. You read way too many books. I think you finally cracked tonight."

"I didn't make this up!" I protested. "I haven't cracked. I know what I saw! His Mr. Winky was out, and he had something tied around his neck. The whole thing was scary and wrong."

Juliet furrowed her brow and stared at me. She opened her mouth and closed it again without speaking. She sat for a few more minutes and then said, "I want to see him."

"I don't want to go back in there." I shivered despite the late September warmth. I hugged my arms around my chest and shook my head. "No way! Whoever killed him might still be in there! You could be their next victim."

"I doubt they stuck around after hearing you stumbling over things in the dark. If someone was there, I am sure they are long gone by now. You don't have to go in with me. I'll check it out and make sure you didn't leave any evidence. Once I'm done, we'll make an anonymous call to the police and *voila!* Problem solved."

"What if you get caught?" I asked. "You're too pretty to go to jail and become Betty Lou Brickhouse's girlfriend."

"I won't get caught. Give me your gloves and tell me how you got in the house. I'll be there and back before you can say shenanigans three times."

"I went in through the back window, but I left through the door in the kitchen. It's unlocked and sitting wide open. I'm sure that's how the killer left, too. I just carried my penlight." I slipped my kid gloves off and passed them to her. She forced her long thin fingers into my small gloves stretching them past the point I could wear them again. I handed her my light.

"If the gloves don't fit, you must acquit!" Juliet joked. She opened the door and slipped out into the darkness.

Twelve long minutes later, she returned and hopped back in Velma. My usually confident sister looked a little paler. Her cocky smile was gone and replaced with a tight-lipped frown.

"Let's go," she said. She took off the gloves and threw them down. She slumped down in the seat.

"Where to?" I shifted Velma into drive, eased away from the curb and drove down the deserted street.

"Head to the Quickie Cow," Juliet replied. "They still have an outside payphone. They closed about a half an hour ago so no one should see us. I think you're right. Someone killed Huey Long."

CHAPTER FOUR

I pulled Velma into the Quickie Cow and parked behind the building so no one could spot us. The Quickie Cow passes for fast food here in Miller's Cove. It was an old Silverstream trailer converted into a kitchen with a counter. A few tables with umbrellas sat on a wooden deck attached on the side and back. It served the best jalapeno burgers and thickest peach shakes in the state. More importantly, there was a payphone in the parking lot. Bless Ma Bell for her invention and forgetting it was still here.

"What should I say?" I asked Juliet as I dug around for change in my leather messenger bag that doubled as my purse. I pulled out two quarters to call the sheriff.

"Don't tell them who you are. Try to disguise your voice and say there's a dead body at 325 Oakwyn Street," Juliet instructed. "Don't give out any more information than you have to and get off the phone fast. We need time to drive home before they send someone to Huey's or here if they trace the call."

I slipped my now too large gloves onto my hands and stepped out. I dropped the quarters into the slot and dialed the number for the sheriff. "Miller's Cove Sheriff's Office. How can I help you?" A deep voice I recognized answered. My stomach dropped into my hobbit-sized feet then flew back up into my throat.

I gulped and squeaked out, "I'd like to report a dead

body."

"And your name?" Asked the voice that used to make my heart go pitter patter every day in high school, college, grad school... Oh, heck. Who was I kidding? Every single day since he befriended my brother Rick when I was ten years old. It was Clint Mason.

"The body can be found at 325 Oakwyn Street. Mr. Huey Long," I stammered out and started to hang up.

"Ophelia Jefferson? Is that you? Phee?" Clint demanded. I slammed down the phone and ran back to the van. I started Velma and drove like my mom on her way to a Black Friday sale at Macy's. My hands were clammy inside the leather gloves and sweat dripped off of me.

"Well?" Juliet asked.

"It was Clint. He recognized my voice when I said where they could find the body." I inhaled deeply and tried to calm down. A glance at my speedometer made me realize I was going 55 in a 35 M.P.H. zone. I eased my foot off the pedal. "Busted. At least my orange jumpsuit will remind me of Velma while I am in the big house filing callouses off some hardened bank robber's heels and being her bunk time wife." I turned into the driveway of my 1920s bungalow and parked.

"Phee, you won't go to jail. You went over there to pick up the books and found the door open. When you stumbled across his body, you panicked and left. You realized it was wrong to leave the scene of the crime, so you pulled into the Quickie Cow and called to report it. Everyone in town knows you. You're so honest you make Abe Lincoln look like a pathological liar. You've got this, so chill the heck out," Juliet said. "One more thing. My car is still a block from the crime scene which isn't good. You need to get me over there pronto so I can move Ole Blue."

I restarted Velma and drove the two miles back to Juliet's convertible. An instantly recognizable convertible guaranteed to give us away if we didn't burn rubber and leave. No sirens, and the streets seemed deserted. Clint might think it was a prank call. Juliet and I drinking one too many gin rickeys on our weekly girls' night out.

"I'll follow you back to your house," Juliet said. "I need a drink and you definitely need one. See you back at your place in just a few minutes." She hopped out and walked to her car.

I once again headed down the road and turned onto Willow Street towards my home. As I pulled up, I saw a truck sitting in my driveway. Leaning against the side of it and talking on his cell phone was Deputy Clint Mason.

CHAPTER FIVE

If I was smart, I would keep driving and act like I didn't see him. Instead, I put on my big girl granny panties and pulled in next to him. I hopped out of Velma and tried to stroll casually towards him. Not an easy task with a dead body on my mind and a sexy deputy sheriff in my driveway.

Clint had wavy dark brown hair and the greenest eyes. His six-foot frame towered over my five foot two self. Every time I saw him, I felt like a silly schoolgirl. I knew he saw me as Rick's little sister, not Ophelia Jefferson, Super Librarian. One day I hoped his hands would undress me in real life instead of just my fantasies.

"Hi, Clint. What's up?" I asked in a nonchalant voice. I continued past him and unlocked my door.

"Really?" Clint's incredulous response told me the game was up. He clipped his phone back into the case on his belt. "Oh, I don't know. You make an anonymous phone call to the sheriff's reporting Huey Long dead in his house and you want to ask me what's up? You're killing me." He strode up the steps and brushed past me into the house. "You want to tell me what crazy stunt you are up to now?"

"I don't do crazy stunts, thank you very much." I tried to sound indignant, but I was so nervous my voice cracked.

"If it's not a girl's night out prank you and Juliet

14

cooked up, then what in the Sam Hill is going on?" He fixed me with an intense glare. When I didn't immediately cave and confess, he sighed. We walked into my kitchen. He opened the refrigerator and pulled out a pitcher of iced tea. Even though he spent time at my home growing up, I felt an intimate domesticity with him right then. Despite the trauma of the evening, I couldn't help but appreciate how good his rear end looked in his khakis. Good googly moogly, he was fine. "Spill it, Phee. I want you to tell me why in the world you made an anonymous call to report a body. You realize a false police report is a punishable crime." Clint reached into the cupboard and pulled out two glasses. He turned and leaned against the counter waiting for an answer.

I took a deep breath and told him I went to Huey Long's house and discovered him naked and dead in the middle of his living room. I left out the part about me mooning the world when my pants came off. I felt some things should be kept secret. Besides it wasn't relevant to the case, darn it!

"Let me see if I understand this. You broke into his house, found his body and decided not to call an ambulance. You presumed he was dead? Ah, Phee, you've put me in a bad spot." I refused to look at him. If I did, I would burst into tears and end up splotchy, snotty and not potential hot girlfriend material.

"I didn't presume anything. Trust me. He was dead. An ambulance wouldn't have changed anything, and I panicked! I've never seen a body. It is way different in real life than when you read about it in an Agatha Christie novel. Clint, I am sorry. Please don't arrest me!" I begged and felt the tears welling in my eyes. In one quick move, he was across the room and pulling me out of the chair and into his arms.

"Don't cry, Flea. No arrests. I promise. I think I know you fairly well and chances are good that you aren't a murderer. Rick would kill me if I arrested you, then your dear, sweet mother would bury me in her vegetable patch. The handcuffs are staying put for now." He ruffled my strawberry blonde curls like I was still twelve years old and following him around asking for a ride on his dirt bike. Unlike Rick's other friends, Clint always found a few minutes to talk before riding off with my brother to "pick up chicks."

"Thanks," I sniffled. "Don't call me, Flea. You know I hate that name."

I pulled myself away from him and poured two glasses of tea for us. To compose myself, I took my time adding sugar to my glass. "Thanks for not thinking I'm a murderess. I would not do well in prison. Orange clashes with my hair."

"You're not off the hook yet. Drink your tea and let's head over to the scene. We need to meet Deputy Thompson. Just in case you weren't joking, I sent him over there to check out things. I got a call from him right before you pulled up. He verified Huey Long is dead. He said it looks like murder."

CHAPTER SIX

Fifteen minutes later, we pulled in behind a patrol car. I spotted yellow crime scene tape circling the yard. My vision grayed, and I felt a little light-headed. Huey Long was dead, and I was involved in a criminal investigation. I grasped the door handle and steadied myself. I took a deep breath. If Miss Marple could handle a crime scene, Ophelia Jefferson could. I walked towards the house with a determined, yet innocent, look on my face. At least I hoped I looked innocent.

"Whoa! Cool your engines there, Phee." Clint grasped my arm to stop me. "I need you to take me step-by-step through your movements. I want to exclude anything belonging to you. But first I need to go talk to Mark and see what he's discovered inside the house. Right now you should get back in the truck and wait for me to come get you. Understand?"

I nodded my head and climbed back in the passenger side. I wasn't going to argue with him at this point. Why poke the bear when the bear was already awake and hungry. The short reprieve gave me time to steady my nerves. I wasn't looking forward to seeing the body again.

The Addams Family theme song boomed out in the truck cab. Startled, I hit my head on the window. I cursed and rummaged in my messenger bag for my cell phone.

"Where are you?" Juliet hissed at me.

"Thanks for abandoning me," I answered. "I thought you were following me to my house. I turn around and no Juliet. I did find Clint standing in my driveway waiting for me. Nice back up, Juls!"

"I did follow you. I followed you and kept right on driving when I saw you and Clint heading into the house. What's going on? You answered your phone, so I guess you aren't in cuffs. Let me know if I need to go ask Mom and Dad for bail money. Glad it's you and not me who needs it. How much do you think bail for murder is? One million? Two?" Juliet could never be serious. I could be bleeding to death on the side of the road and somehow she'd find a way to crack a joke.

"Ha ha. Funny. Do not say a word to anyone about this. Remember that I know where you live and have a key to your apartment. You breathe a word, and I will replace your tie-dye with polyester! I didn't tell Clint you met me at the crime scene. As far as he knows, it was me all by my lonesome and let's keep it that way. If Mom and Dad find out about this they will kill me. Better only one of us is in jail. Someone needs to stay free to feed Ferdie. I'm at Huey's house waiting to go through things with Clint and Deputy Thompson. Go home and keep your lips zipped. If you spill the beans, I'll tell everyone all about your weekend stay in the county clink when you went to Florida for spring break," I threatened. "I'll call you tomorrow morning and give you an update. Remember what I said. Not a word."

"Sheesh. Give the threats of non-cotton clothing a rest. I won't say anything. I'm not the one who broke into a house under dark of night with a mask on, my jail bird sister. I am an innocent bystander," Juliet said. "Just teasing. All kidding aside, I love you, Flea. If you need me, call and I promise I'll be there." She hung up before I could respond. Juliet might be a bit of a granola-eating hippie, but I knew she would stand right by my side in a fight. I tucked the phone back into my bag. I glanced up and saw Clint striding towards the truck. He did not look happy. In fact, he appeared downright grim. I stepped out and headed his way.

"I need you to walk me through from the time you left Velma until the time you got back into her," Clint said as he walked up next to me. We headed towards the backyard. He turned on his large flashlight and skimmed it over scene.

"I came through Mrs. Grimes' yard and then walked up to the window right there." I pointed to the window with the squashed tulips. Huey prided himself on his beautiful flower beds. I felt a pang of remorse for stepping on them. "The window was open a crack. I pushed it up and climbed through." I reached over to demonstrate. He grabbed my hand to stop me.

"Hold on! Touch nothing. What is that caught on the window?" He reached over and plucked red fabric from the frame. He held it up to inspect it under his flashlight. I felt a crimson tide wash over me as I realized it was a piece of the red lace thong I wore. I guess I caught more than just my pants when I got stuck.

"Um... that's from me. I, uh, accidentally caught myself on the frame as I climbed in," I stammered.

"Your pants are black." Clint peered down at me

19

with a grin on his face. "When did you find time to change?"

"Those are from my panties if you must know. My pants came off because I my rear wouldn't quite fit when I tried to squeeze through," I said with as much dignity as I could muster. Please let the great god of sinkholes take pity on me and suck me into the bowels of the earth right now.

"I'll make a note of that in my report." His eyes twinkling, he walked towards the back door and motioned for me to follow. "I don't want you to climb back through the window and moon Deputy Thompson. Let's use the door, okay?"

"Thanks," I said. I tossed my hair to look like a composed and cool woman rather than nervous murder suspect. I marched through the door and towards the living room. I stopped when I saw Deputy Thompson leaning over the body.

"Well, Ms. Jefferson, you landed yourself in a heap of trouble tonight." Deputy Mark Thompson first met me when I begged him to take me to a crime scene so I could try out my Junior Girl Detective Kit. I was eight years old then. Twenty years later and he finally let me behind the crime scene tape. He'd retired a few years ago but realized fishing wasn't enough to keep him occupied and out of his wife's hair, so he returned to work part-time. At least it was Mark investigating me and not Sheriff Dawes, my dad's close friend. I would be mortified if Dad found out about my escapade tonight.

"Hey there, Mark." I smiled weakly at him. "It's

nice to see you but not very nice to be here next to a dead body."

"What's the verdict, Mark?" Clint knelt down next to the body. Now that the lights were on in the house, I could see a belt buckled tightly around Huey's neck causing his eyes to bulge. His Mr. Winky was now standing at half-mast. I felt queasy at the sight of him.

"Based on what I've found so far, someone strangled him. We'll wait for Doc to make the official determination though. His laptop was open on the desk and from what I saw he had some interesting taste in porn. Don't you look over there, Ms. Jefferson. Ladies shouldn't look at that kind of trash. The killer must have walked in the unlocked back door and somehow sneaked up on him while he was at the desk. I saw some scuff marks in the carpet. They must have dragged him over here and laid him out. I also found some footprints in the dirt next to the back door. I marked it with an evidence flag and took a photo. Whoever was standing out there was wearing a pair of sneakers. It looks to be a small-sized shoe. I'm not sure what brand."

"Thanks, Mark. Phee, did you touch anything in the room? See or hear anything when you were in here?" Clint interrogated me.

"No. I was wearing gloves. I touched the library books I came to get. I'm sure that was it. It was dark and with my little penlight, I really couldn't see much." I felt my gaze drawn back to Huey. At that moment, I wished I hadn't listened to Juliet. I should have stayed a nice girl with her nose buried in her books.

CHAPTER SEVEN

The next morning I crawled my way into work clutching the largest coffee I could buy at Nellie Jo's Cup o' Joe. My eyes felt gritty and my brain filled with sand. I was a girl who needed eight hours of sleep to even pass for human. Glancing up at me as I came behind the circulation desk, Wade, my part-time clerk, tech guru and occasional janitor, turned the front page of the newspaper towards me.

"You look like crap. Did you see this? Someone killed that jerk, Huey Long. Good riddance, I say. The man was a walking billboard advertising trouble." Wade was ex-Army and not known for mincing his words. "Every time he came in here and opened his mouth, I wanted to drop kick his little ass right back out to the curb."

"I found the body!" I blurted it out before I could stop myself. So much for my plan of not letting anybody know. Clint would kill me. He promised to keep my name out of the newspaper. I should take out a front page ad in the newspaper and tell everyone. There was a good reason Juliet often accused me of having diarrhea of the mouth. I wasn't good at keeping secrets. This secret was so big, it was begging to be let out.

"Say what? How in the heck did you find him? He was killed in his home according to the paper, and I know he wasn't high on your list of prospective dating partners. What was it you said? I think it was something like 'I would rather burn my eyeballs out with a hot iron poker than date that evil little man.' But I guess I misunderstood," Wade smirked at me.

"You and my sister, Juliet, ought to form a comedy team. She thinks she's hilarious, too. For your information, I went there to get our books he refused to bring back or pay for, thank you very much. I found him dead and called the sheriff's office." I snatched the paper from him, settled onto a stool and sipped my coffee.

"Wow! The article said the cause of death appeared to be strangulation, but they aren't releasing any more details right now. Tell me everything that the newspaper isn't saying. Remember, we have ways of making you talk. Mwahaha!" Wade threatened while giving his best impression of an evil interrogator. He set down the mail he was sorting and peered at me. "Spill it, Phee!"

"Not much else to tell. His back door was open, so I went in. I found him strangled and got out of there as fast as I could in case the murderer was still there. I called the sheriff's office. End of story." There was no way I would tell anyone what else I saw - Huey Long in his birthday suit.

Clint had threatened me with everything short of death if I blabbed. My mouth would remain shut if I had to put duct tape across it. He would be angry I told Wade as much as I had.

"You're lucky you weren't hurt. What were you thinking going over there by yourself? First, Huey Long was an ass. Second, no book is worth you getting molested by the troll. If you wanted someone to go crack some kneecaps and do collections, you should've taken me with you." Wade cracked his knuckles in his best imitation of a mafia hit man.

"I waited until I knew he'd be out of his house. I just planned on sneaking in, grabbing the books and leaving. I didn't expect to find him there. Dead or alive. You know he always does karaoke on Thursday nights. I thought I would be perfectly safe. In and out in five minutes. Problem solved. Now, I'm a witness in a murder." I sipped my coffee and wrapped one of my red curls around my finger attempting to look casual. "Clint Mason is the investigator on the case."

"You're not telling me everything. You always twist your hair when you lie. I know you too well, boss lady." He rolled out from behind the desk. He grabbed the books off the cart and headed into the stacks to shelve them. "And please stop mooning over Clint and just tell him."

"Nothing to tell," I murmured under my breath. "And I'm not lying!" I said the last bit loud enough for Wade. I heard him laugh as he rolled down the aisle between the shelves.

For the rest of the day, I tried to make myself scarce by dusting and shelving all the books rather than work at the desk. Wade worked at circulation and stayed busy checking people's books out to them. The murder was the only thing anyone could talk about.

"Hey there, pretty lady. Did you hear the big news?" Startled, I dropped the DVDs I was shelving.

"Hi, Cincinnati. Yes, I heard about the murder. It's

all anyone wants to talk about today," I said resignedly. I knew I'd be dragged into the gossip eventually.

"Murder? I'm talking about the Reds being named Wilson Defensive Team of the Year. That's the news I'm talking about!" Charlie "Cincinnati" Cochran was a regular visitor at the Miller's Cove Library. He came daily to read the paper and talk sports with anyone who would listen. I tried to tell him I didn't know diddly about baseball. He always continued to describe each play of every game played by his favorite team, the Cincinnati Reds.

Charlie had been the town's head groundskeeper for the parks and public greens for years until he retired five years ago. Since then, he followed a daily routine. He hit Nellie Jo's Cup o' Joe first thing. Then he would meander his way towards the library before heading towards the senior center for lunch and a game of chess. He was getting up in years. Last winter he had taken a nasty fall on the ice and broken his shoulder. Charlie never married and had no family, so we all tried to keep an eye out for him.

"That's awesome. Bet that made your day." I leaned down to pick up the DVDs I dropped. "The only thing anyone else is talking about is the murder of Huey Long."

"That bag of wind. I can't say I'm sorry. I didn't like the way he grabbed you the other day. Made me want to kick him right in his behind!" Charlie made a kicking motion and grinned at me. "You can count on old Charlie here to look out for you."

I patted Charlie on his arm and told him I would talk

to him later. For the rest of the afternoon, I hid myself in my office. I attempted to get some paperwork done in my office until time to go home. People were exhausting.

At five o'clock, Wade announced the library was closed. He shut down the computers and locked the door behind the last patron. I saw him wince when he caught his hand between the desk and his chair and felt a twinge of guilt. Wade's Humvee rolled over an IED outside of Fallujah. He lost both of his legs, but he never complained. Wade was the only one of his team who had survived. He came home from Walter Reed Hospital a year ago and asked me for a job. He didn't need the money but needed to be busy to keep his demons at bay. I paid him a pittance from my meager budget, but he didn't care. He said the books in the library allowed him to travel to places "a helluva lot better than that hot ass sandbox I was in."

"I can lock up if you want to head out of here," I offered.

"I'll take you up on that offer. I've got a smoking hot date tonight, so I need time to wax my ride." He attempted a leer.

I shooed him out of the building. I finished turning everything off and headed out the door. As I walked to Velma, I heard someone call my name. Turning, I spotted Carla Karsen tottering on her three-inch heels down the sidewalk towards me. I groaned. I avoided Carla like the plague. As the former head cheerleader at Miller's Cove High, she had roamed the halls with her pack of friends terrorizing everyone outside of her clique, including me. Although it was years ago, my

DEATH IS LONG OVERDUE

blood still boiled every time I saw her. As a council member, she spoke out against the library at every town hall meeting. She wanted to tear down the 120-year-old building and replace it with a recreation center and pool. Her plan was to make a "reading room for the few people who still read the old-fashioned way." I don't think she had cracked a book since reading *Fox in Socks* when she was five.

She glared at me as she teetered up. "I think we need to talk before the next town council meeting. My idea will draw more young people and money to the downtown area of Miller's Cove. People don't read books anymore, Ophelia. They can find all they need on the internet. You need to realize that my idea is what this town needs. I plan to help the town grow. It will encourage more families to relocate here which means more business for everyone. I'd be happy to have you come and work at the new fitness center. We could always use someone to help clean the pool."

"Carla, I'm sure that in your mind you're convinced that you're right, but the rest of the town council doesn't agree. If you ever tried to read a book…" I trailed off before I stuck my foot any further into my mouth. I disliked Carla with a passion. She always made me feel awkward. It didn't matter I was an educated, professional woman. Whenever Carla came around me, I felt like the same fifteen-year-old girl with bad hair and braces. She hadn't been an ugly duckling like me, and she used her looks to her advantage every chance she could.

"Listen, you little witch, you think you are so damn smart. Mark my words, I will get my way. When I do, I

27

will make sure you never find another job in this town."
She poked me in the chest with her pointy, hot pink
nails.

"Hey there, pretty lady. You're coming to the
concert over at the high school tonight, aren't you?"
Cincinnati walked over and stood next to me. Carla
huffed and backed away from me.

"Not tonight, Charlie." I was grateful for the
interruption.

"I'll talk to you later," Carla threatened. She spun on
her heels and tottered on down the sidewalk.

"You looked like you needed rescuing there, Phee.
You okay?" Charlie asked.

"Thanks, Charlie. I'm fine. Just tired and ready to go
home. I'll see you tomorrow." I turned back towards
my van and climbed in.

"You have any more problems with that one," he
said pointing down the sidewalk at Carla's retreating
back, "you let me know. She's a piece of work. One of
these days, she is going to get in the wrong person's
face."

"I will. Thanks again. Have a good evening." I fired
up Velma and pointed her towards home, a hot cup of
tea, and much needed peace and quiet.

CHAPTER EIGHT

I walked through my front door and a loud meow echoed from the kitchen. Ferdinand was waiting for his dinner and made sure I realized he was not a happy fat cat. Once I had filled his fish-shaped bowl with chow, I put the kettle on the stove to boil. I opened my vintage turquoise refrigerator to scrounge for something to eat. I grabbed a bag of romaine lettuce, an avocado and some leftover chicken and threw together a quick salad. The teapot whistled. As I turned off the burner, my phone trilled.

"Hello?" I answered and stretched the phone cord over to the counter so I could make some peppermint tea and prepare my salad.

"Hi, honey. It's Mom," said my mother like I wouldn't recognize her voice after twenty-eight years. "Did you hear the news? Huey Long was murdered in his home!"

Sighing, I stirred honey into my tea. I nestled the phone onto my shoulder and carried my plate and mug to my turquoise Formica table. I settled onto a matching vinyl chair. "Yes. It was the hot newsflash that everyone talked about at work today. No one had anything nice to say about Mr. Long. He was a jerk."

"Well, some crazed person strangled him. Sheila told me," Mom lowered her voice, "he was in his birthday suit." Mom didn't need to read the newspaper. She got the news through her bridge game. Sheriff Dawes' wife,

Sheila, played cards with my mom every week.

"Hmmm…well, that's news to me." There was no way I would tell my parents I broke into a house in a disguise and stumbled over a corpse. "What time do I need to be there next Sunday? Do you want me to bring anything?"

"Five sharp and it would be nice if you brought a date." My mother recently resorted to dropping hints she and Dad weren't getting any younger and would love to see my sister and I settle down and have children. My brother Rick was expecting twins with his wife, Carrie. Juliet believed the babies' pending arrival would keep her from pestering us. The steam engine called Mom had slowed but not stopped.

"I don't have a date to bring, Mom, so I guess I'll just bring dessert," I responded dryly. I sneaked a bite of salad and held the phone away from my mouth while I chewed. "Who else is coming to the party?"

"Your brother and Carrie, Clint and his date, and Uncle Joe and Aunt Sarah are coming. Uncle Paul might drive down, but he's not sure. A bunch of other people called and said they planned to attend. I need to call the caterer tomorrow with the final count," Mom said.

"Clint's bringing a date?" My heart sank a little. There were no rumblings through the rumor mill about a new woman in Clint's life, but I also hadn't asked.

"Well, I assume he is. I told him to bring someone. I know he broke up with Simone a few weeks ago, but the word is he is interested in someone new," Mom continued. She was oblivious to my heartbreak over her news.

Abruptly I said, "I'm sorry, Mom, but I need to go. My dinner is getting cold. I'll see you on Sunday. Love you."

"Love you, too, honey."

I trudged across my black and white tile floor to hang the phone up. I don't know why I was surprised or upset that Clint was interested in someone new. Clint Mason was handsome and had a great sense of humor. He was just an all-around nice guy. Every single woman in town tried to catch his eye. His only fault was that he went through girlfriends like I went through a bag of chocolate chip cookies. Fast. His most recent girlfriend, Simone, was an attorney from Burlington. I liked her because she was smart, accomplished, and pretty without being bitchy. Not that I wasn't glad that Clint wasn't with her. I just wished I could figure out how to make him realize I was a grown woman and not a kid anymore. I speared some chicken and lettuce onto a fork.

"Ferdie, my friend," I said to him as he coiled in and out of my chair legs, "it is time for me to realize that Clint is not interested in me and move on. You and I just need to get over him and get a life." I washed my few dishes and dried my hands on a vintage days-of-the-week tea towel. Perhaps I should bring my own date to the party on Sunday. Well if I could even find someone to go with me. It's not like Miller's Cove was a dating hot spot. It was time I put away the fantasies and started living in the real world. "But before I do that," I reached down and picked up Ferdie to carry him with me, "let's watch *Roman Holiday* one more time."

I changed into my flannel pajamas covered with sheep dressed in various cocktail dresses holding glasses of wine. My feet sported my favorite skunk slippers and my unruly curls had been pulled into a ponytail on the top of my head. I grabbed a quilt in varying shades of blue that my grandmother made for me before she died. Ferdie trailed behind me as I walked to my living room and settled onto my 1920s chaise lounge. The only concession to the modern age in the living room was my television and DVD player which I tastefully hid in one of the many built-in mahogany bookcases. I loved my house. Each room was decorated in a style from the early half of the 20th century. My lack of social life had one perk. It gave me plenty of time to hunt through the antique stores searching for the perfect pieces to add to my home. Hitting play on the remote control, the opening theme song played, and I snuggled into my blanket.

Right as I got comfortable, my doorbell buzzed. I stood up and walked into the foyer to peek through the side window before opening the door. It was Clint, and I was in flannel sheep pajamas and skunk slippers. Great. But what did I care? I had moved on only a few minutes ago. Donning a steely eyed librarian look, I opened the door.

"Hey there, Flea," Clint said. A slow smile spread across his face as his green eyes took in my fashion ensemble. He wasn't good looking in a movie star perfect looks kind of way. He was ruggedly handsome. Clint looked like a cowboy who worked hard and spent time out on the range roping calves and sleeping next to a campfire. A slightly crooked nose was from the time, my brother broke it during a rough and tumble football match amongst the neighborhood kids. Instead of marring his looks, it added to them. He had a little dimple in his chin my mother always said was where an angel had kissed him when he was born.

"I told you to quit calling me Flea! You may not realize it, but I'm not twelve years old anymore. Here's a news flash. Ophelia Jefferson is a twenty-eight-year-old woman. An adult!" I glowered at him. "What do you want?"

"A little touchy tonight, aren't you? Those sheep pajamas and slippers scream twelve years old, but I like them. They are most definitely you. I just came to give you an update on the case. Can I come inside?" Clint asked. I opened the door wider and motioned him inside. He wasn't in his uniform. Instead, he wore some old faded jeans, a pair of dusty cowboy boots and a forest green shirt that made his eyes appear even greener. My heart beat a little faster.

"I was just getting ready to watch a movie. Come on into the kitchen while I make some popcorn." I walked with as much dignity as I could muster while little skunk tails trailed behind my feet. I opened the cupboard and pulled out a pan. After pouring some oil into it, I placed it on the stove. "Would you like something to drink?"

"Do you have any coffee? It's been a long day, and I am beat." He settled onto one of my kitchen chairs. I scooped coffee into my Sunbeam percolator.

"Why do you do that?" Clint asked. I plugged in the pot. I grabbed a bag of popcorn as the oil in the pan sizzled. Placing one kernel of corn in the pan, I waited for it to pop.

"Do what?" I asked. The kernel soon popped up and out of the pan. I hurried and poured more corn in and covered the pan with a lid. The pings of the kernels as they exploded inside the pan echoed throughout the kitchen. I shook the pan to keep them from burning.

"Why is everything in your house old? A percolator instead of a new coffeepot. An old refrigerator. Why make popcorn on the stove instead of in the microwave like the rest of the world?" Clint gestured towards the stove.

"I guess I just like vintage things. Everything in the world moves too fast these days. I think that's why I love books so much, too. Everyone wants things to be like a sitcom. They want instant gratification and their problems solved in 30 minutes. In novels, you get to know the characters and become invested in their lives. The stories take time to develop. You can put the book down and come back to it later and be in that world again. With TV, once that half hour or hour is over, that's it. Things that take time just seem better." I shrugged and gave the pan a last shake and pulled it off the stove. The percolator gave its final perk. I poured coffee into the mugs and placed one on the table in front of Clint. He took a slow sip.

"You might be right about the coffee at least. This is the best cup I've had in a long time." He settled back into his seat and took another sip. "The preliminary results are in on Huey Long which is why I am here. Estimated time of death was around 5 p.m. It puts you in the clear since half the town saw you leaving the library with Juliet at five o'clock. Everyone in town knows you always have dinner at Mimi's Restaurant with your sister on Thursday night."

"Great. I'm glad my boring, predictable life gives me an alibi," I said as I dumped the popcorn in a bowl. I grabbed a few pieces and popped them into my mouth. Delicious. There was nothing better than fresh popped popcorn.

"You're not boring, Phee. You are dependable, and you care about your family. That's a good thing," Clint replied and grabbed a handful of popcorn as I sat down next to him.

"What about his... you know... his..." I blushed as I tried to ask about Huey's state when I found him.

Clint smiled at my discomfort. "Well, yes. There's that. It seems Huey Long had an online love affair with a woman in the Ukraine. They had a standing "date" night on Thursday which accounts for him being naked. As for the other thing, we found a newly filled bottle of Viagra in the bathroom with three pills missing. It appears he wanted to last an extra-long time for Natasha. We found quite a bit of information through his internet chat history and his credit card bill with a repeated $250 charge every Thursday to Hot Ukrainian Chicks dot com. Unfortunately, some nuggets of knowledge about Huey and his sex life are never going to leave my brain. Mark and I may need therapy after some of the things we saw on that computer. Anyway, that's all we know for now but at least that puts you in the clear. I may have to arrest you for killing skunks out of season to make those slippers though."

"Funny. That's pretty disgusting about Huey and his internet love affair. I need to purge that picture from my mind. Thanks for sharing it. Huey Long and his lady love doing a computer sex chat. Gross!" I shook my head trying to shake the image from my mind. "But I am glad I'm not a suspect. Do you have any possible suspects to even interrogate?"

"Not right now. Well, I've had enough talk about Huey and his creepy computer habits for the night. What movie are you watching?" Clint asked as he snagged another handful of popcorn and tossed pieces one by one into his mouth.

"*Roman Holiday* with Audrey Hepburn. It's my all-time favorite," I replied.

"Never seen it," Clint admitted.

"What? You're kidding me! How have you managed to miss out on one of the greatest classic movies ever made? You need to watch it." I popped another piece of popcorn into my mouth.

"Is that an invitation?" He grinned at me.

"You can stay, but you can't talk during the movie. It's my biggest pet peeve!" I warned. My heart skipped a beat in anticipation of Clint cuddling on the couch with me while watching a romantic film.

He grabbed up the bowl of popcorn and headed towards the living room. He settled onto the old leather couch. Not wanting to be too bold, I sat back down on my chaise lounge. I told myself that this was just him being nice to a girl he considered his little sister. Secretly, though, my heart was dancing an Irish jig of joy. I was doing cartwheels of delight in my brain. I restarted the movie and the theme song continued from where I had stopped it. A few minutes later, I heard a gentle chuffing sound from the couch. Clint had fallen asleep. I grabbed the throw I had on the back of the couch and covered him up. Poor guy must be exhausted from the long day. I watched him sleep for a minute, then I smiled and settled back to enjoy Audrey Hepburn and Gregory Peck falling in love.

I awoke to Clint placing a blanket over me. The television was playing *The Star Spangled Banner* with a flag waving in the background. The movie must have ended hours ago.

"What're you doing?" I mumbled through a sleepy yawn. "What time is it?"

"I've got to get home, Phee. You go back to sleep, and I'll see you tomorrow," Clint whispered. I snuggled deeper into the covers and felt myself dozing. A moment later, the front door opened and closed. Before he left me, I could have sworn Clint kissed me on my head. It must have been a dream, so I drifted back to sleep.

CHAPTER NINE

I awoke Saturday morning to two bright green eyes inches from my face. Unfortunately, they were not the green eyes of Clint but of the grumpy, twenty-five pound cat sitting on my chest waiting for his breakfast kibbles. Who needs an alarm clock when they have a cat with a bottomless stomach and no boundaries?

I stretched, patted Ferdie and gently pushed him to the floor. I got up and walked to the kitchen to feed him and start my morning coffee.

It was my Saturday to work. I hurried to jump in the shower while my coffee perked and burbled away on the counter. My bathroom was a glorious flamingo pink with black accents. Even the toilet was pink. As I dried myself off, I inspected my face in the gilt mirror over the sink. I had long, strawberry-blonde curls and unlike some redheads, only a light dusting of freckles across the bridge of my nose. My gray eyes sometimes appeared blue depending on what I wore. I had my dad's coloring and my mother's short, curvy build. Maybe I wouldn't win a beauty contest, but I wouldn't kick myself out of the bed.

I dressed in a comfortable pair of jeans since Saturday was also the day when most of the weekly cleaning at the library took place. I pulled a bright blue ribbed turtleneck over my head and added a long strand of freshwater pearls with matching earrings. I slipped my feet into a pair of black clogs and clomped back to the kitchen. The percolator stopped perking while I was in the shower, so I filled my Joe-to-go mug with hot coffee and added cream, sugar and just a hint of a cinnamon nutmeg mix in honor of the brisk fall weather. I smeared a bagel with some cream cheese and headed out the door.

When I pulled up to the library, I spotted Cincinnati sitting outside waiting for me to open the doors. On the Saturdays that I opened up, I let him come in early with me. He kept me company, and he helped empty all the garbage cans.

"Morning, Charlie!" I gave him a cheerful wave. I unlocked the doors. Once we were in the building, I locked the doors behind us. We still had about fifteen minutes until opening.

"Morning," Charlie responded in a grumpy voice. He went over to the garbage can next to the door and pulled the bag out. He was always cheerful when he came in, so his dour expression was unusual for him.

"What's the matter?" I asked as I turned on all the lights and then switched on all the computers. "You aren't your usual smiley self. You haven't given me one baseball fact this morning. Are you sick?"

"Aw, it's nothing," he replied. He headed behind the circulation desk to grab the trash. "I just ran into that Carla Karsen outside a bit before you got here. She was going on and on about how nice a fitness center would be. She said some people could do with some more exercise instead of sitting and reading a book all day. It just made me angry."

"I wouldn't worry about it. She might think that no

one reads books anymore, but I think we can definitely prove her wrong. We have at least a hundred people come here every day. The kids in this town all love our programs and our reading contests. The town council would be idiots to close the library to build a recreation center with just a reading room. Besides, there are other locations in this town where Carla could build. She's just jealous because I exercise my brain and she doesn't."

"I know it and you know it, but she doesn't care. If Carla has her way, she would get this building torn down and finagle a honey of a deal from the rest of the council. Somebody needs to stop her." Charlie slammed down the empty can and headed out the back door to put the bag in the outside bin. He was right about Carla and her plans. I still thought I didn't have too much to worry about though. Carla was like a mosquito that buzzed from victim to victim looking for blood. The thing about mosquitoes was they either went away or got squashed. Too bad neither happened with Carla.

At ten o'clock sharp, I opened the doors. Charlie left to attend the fire department's benefit breakfast. I stayed busy throughout the morning doing some family tree research for Mrs. Young. At noon, my other part-timer, Claire, came in. She was a high school student who loved books. She was quiet and did a great job. Sometimes I found her sitting on the floor somewhere immersed in a book when she was supposed to be shelving. I always let Claire continue reading. When I was a helper here as a teenager, the former librarian would shake her head at me and give me a knowing smile whenever she caught me hiding in a corner with my nose buried in a book.

I was busy cleaning up after one o'clock story time when I felt someone walk up behind me. Standing up, I turned to see Grant Davis. Grant and I were best friends throughout high school. We both competed on the debate team and possessed similar taste in movies, music and books. We lost touch when he left Miller's Cove to attend law school at the University of Iowa. I heard he moved back to town two months ago and joined the law office of Biddle, Smith and Talty.

"Phee Jefferson! It is good to see you," Grant said. He had filled out since his high school years. The extra weight looked good on him. His curly blonde hair that had given him a cherubic appearance in his youth was brushed back and he sported a mustache. It was a good style for him. I gave him a warm hug.

"Gosh! You look great. I knew you were back in town, but I didn't have a chance to hunt you down." I smiled at him.

"I got tired of waiting for you to call me. I decided to come down here and check out for myself the rumor you became our town librarian last year."

"For once, the rumor is true. So you became some big shot defense attorney at the local law firm. I guess you aren't doing too badly yourself. I ran into your mom just the other day at the market. She raved about how proud she was of you. She said that she missed us hanging out in the house driving her crazy. I know she's had a hard time since your dad passed away. I bet she's happy to have you home. My mom's been checking on her and tries to take her out to lunch, but she seems to prefer to stay at home most of the time. Mom persuaded her to come here last week for a nature program. I think she enjoyed herself. She actually stayed afterwards to chat with folks," I said.

My mom and Shari Davis became friends ten years ago. They both spent hours driving around town looking for Grant and me when we skipped school one day. We had gone to an all-day marathon of classic movies at the local theater. We were honor roll students, so we hadn't seen the harm in one skip day. Mom and Shari didn't agree with our logic. Our parents grounded us for a month, but our moms had been friends ever since.

"That's part of the reason I came home. I called her every week, but I could tell she was depressed. After a few phone calls, it became apparent to me she was not doing well. She and my dad were soulmates. It is going to take her a long time to recover from his death. If she ever does. I'm all she has left. I called Mr. Biddle Senior, he interviewed me, and well, here I am. Mom and I just got back from the fire department benefit breakfast. She asked me to swing by here so she could turn in her library books. If Mohammed won't come to the mountain, the mountain must come to Mohammed!" I spotted Shari browsing the paperbacks on the other side of the library. I lifted a hand in greeting to her, and she waved back.

"Well, I, for one, am glad you are back. I need my best movie buddy. Juliet only likes horror movies and action films. She refuses to go with me when they do the classics marathon. Speaking of which, they are playing *Gone with the Wind* tonight. We should go!" I

DEATH IS LONG OVERDUE

said excitedly. When we were kids, Grant was always willing to hit the theater with me regardless of what was playing.

"Well, that's another reason I wanted to come by and visit you. Great minds must think alike. I saw that it was playing and immediately thought of you. I've been busy moving and getting settled, and I haven't had a chance to come talk with you yet. So you don't have a hot date already lined up?" Grant asked. He stuffed his hands into his pockets and gave me a hopeful look.

"Nope. It was just going to be me and my cat curled up with a mystery tonight. How about I meet you at the theater about fifteen minutes before the show starts? That will give us time to get our Jujubes and slushies and try to snag our usual seats." It would be nice to get out of the house tonight and not dwell on the past few days.

"I have an even better idea. Why don't I pick you up at seven o'clock and we can have dinner at Mimi's then head over to the theater?" Grant suggested.

"That'll work. My house is the dark green bungalow at 566 Willow Street. You can't miss it. I have an aqua blue and white 1968 VW van parked in the driveway. Listen, it's been great seeing you, but I should get back to work. These books are like gremlins and multiply when you aren't looking. I'll see you at seven." I reached over and gave him another quick hug.

"It's a date." Grant smiled at me, turned and walked away. I paused for a moment at the word date. I shook my head. I was reading too much into it.

Grant and I had been inseparable growing up. While

the other girls in school were busy chasing boys, polishing their nails and gossiping about the latest boy band, I was watching classic movies and reading Jane Austen. Grant's parents were a little older when they adopted him. He seemed to have grown up in a different era than the other kids. We gravitated towards each other. Our friendship was sealed in middle school when Carla and her pack of hyenas "accidentally" dumped a carton of milk on my shirt in the school cafeteria. They had all screeched that I was lactating. I had been mortified. Grant came to my rescue when he yanked off his pullover and offered it to me. We'd been thick as thieves ever since. It was a shame we had lost touch during college.

The rest of the afternoon flew by. I closed up the library at five o'clock and hurried home to change. I chose a midnight blue silk blouse and paired it with my favorite faded jeans and brown riding boots. I spritzed my favorite 1920s perfume, *My Sin*, behind my ears. I flicked some mascara on my eyelashes and added a hint of peach lipstick. The addition of my favorite silver hoop earrings completed the ensemble. I hoped my outfit said "casual night out with a friend."

A few minutes before seven, Grant pulled up to the house. I grabbed my jacket and headed out to meet him.

"I was going to be a gentleman and come to the door," Grant said. He stepped out of his black Porsche 918 Spyder and walked around to open my car door for me. He had changed into a dark blue polo shirt with a black leather jacket.

I gave a low whistle. "Holy cow! You must be doing great to drive a car like this." I settled into the soft leather seats and gave a sigh of pleasure. Grant climbed into the driver's seat, pushed a button and the engine purred like a well-fed cat.

"I do alright. No wife or kids yet, so I decided to buy myself a toy with the money from the new job. I want to play a little before I grow up and settle down." Grant turned down Main Street towards Mimi's. The parking lot next to Mimi's was full since it was a Saturday night.

"I'll drop you off at the front door, drive down and park at the pharmacy. I'll meet you inside," Grant suggested.

"I'll put our name on the list if there's a wait." I climbed out when he pulled up to the curb.

I walked inside and gave the hostess my name. She advised me a table should be ready in about ten minutes and suggested I order a drink. I sat at the bar and ordered a Cosmopolitan while I waited for Grant. As I turned to face the door so I could watch for him, I was surprised to see Clint heading towards the exit. Walking next to him was an attractive brunette. She was almost as tall as he was and voluptuous in all the right places. Turning away so he wouldn't spot me, I attempted to track his movements in the mirror behind the bartender. A moment later, Clint appeared behind me with the woman. She must be the new love interest my mom had mentioned.

"Hi, Phee," Clint greeted me. I turned my stool towards him. In an attempt to appear calm, cool and collected, I took a sip of my drink. I swallowed wrong and ended up coughing and gagging. Clint patted me on the back. "Are you okay?"

"I'm fine. Just went down the wrong pipe," I gasped when I finally caught my breath. I could feel the blush of embarrassment from the roots of my hair all the way to my toes.

"This is Grace Winchester." Clint turned to the brunette. "Grace, this is my friend, Phee Jefferson."

"Nice to meet you, Phee. Is that short for something?" Grace had a low, sultry voice. I instantly hated her a little more for it. The fact that she was gorgeous didn't help.

"It's short for Ophelia. Nice to meet you, too." I gave her a tight smile as I fingered the stem of my glass.

"Grace is here for a few days. I figured she couldn't leave Miller's Cove without trying Mimi's famous coconut cake. Grace is..."

"Were you able to get us a table, Phee?" Grant walked up and interrupted Clint before he could finish. "Clint Mason. Long time, man. How's it going?" Grant shook hands with Clint and then placed an arm around my shoulders.

"I'm doing alright. So what are you two up to this evening?" Clint glanced at Grant's arm around my shoulder. Did I imagine a slight tightening of his expression?

"We were just going to grab a bite to eat before catching the nine o'clock show at the theater. They're playing *Gone with the Wind*, and it's one of Phee's favorite movies," Grant replied. I felt his hand tighten possessively around my shoulder. He leaned a little closer to me. Grant knew all about my teenage crush on Clint, so I wondered what game he was playing.

"Good running into you, Grant. Grace and I should get going and let you enjoy your date. Phee, I'll see you later." Clint turned and taking Grace's elbow, the two of them headed towards the door.

"It's not a date," I said quietly under my breath. "I guess I just met your new love interest though."

"I'm sorry," Grant said. "I couldn't hear you. The music is a little loud."

I smiled at him. "I said that I think a slice of Mimi's famous coconut cake for dessert might be just the thing."

CHAPTER TEN

The next morning was Sunday, and I was a hot mess. I had spent the previous evening ruminating over Clint and his new lady love. Grant sensed something was wrong and tried to draw it out of me, but I told him it had just been a long week and I was tired. To make up for my foul mood, I suggested that he come with his mother to the birthday dinner at my parent's house. He agreed with more enthusiasm than he should have. At the end of the evening, he leant in a little too close. His lips expected a good night kiss which didn't happen and never would. I gave him a brief hug and hurried into my house without inviting him in.

I pulled on my baby blue chenille robe and knotted it around my waist with a sharp tug. I slid my feet into my pink elephant slippers and scuffed my way to the front porch to grab the Sunday edition of the *Miller's Cove Courier*. After feeding Ferdie his Sunday treat of grilled tuna, I poured myself a cup of coffee and settled at the kitchen table to read the newspaper. The headlines blared out in large font, "Local Business Woman Found Dead!" Below the headlines was a photograph of Carla Karsen winning one of her awards as top local real estate agent. Holy cow! I didn't like her, but I didn't want her dead. I read further.

"Local real estate agent, aerobics instructor and town council member, Carla Karsen, died in her home late last night. At around nine o'clock, an ambulance was dispatched after a call came in from Chris Karsen, the victim's husband. Mr. Karsen reported the victim was delirious and violently ill. The ambulance arrived within moments and attempted lifesaving treatment. Mrs. Karsen died before she could be transported to the hospital. Mrs. Karsen's body will undergo an autopsy to determine the cause of death."

I leaned back against my chair and tried to process what I read. Poor Carla. What a horrible way to die and at such a young age. I felt guilty that I had made up a song about her a few weeks ago. I took Paul Simon's *Fifty Ways to Leave Your Lover* and called my tune *Fifty Ways to Kill Old Carla*. Juliet and I chuckled over it for days. Neither one of us cared for Carla. Now, I felt a little ill because I plotted her death in my imagination since high school. With a guilty sigh, I continued to read the paper. Below the headline news was a quarter-page article on the Huey Long murder investigation.

"Police have released further details regarding the death of local resident, Huey Long. Long was strangled in his home sometime around five p.m. on Thursday. Mr. Long had an online appointment at the time. The individual video chatting with him stated the suspect was wearing dark gloves and a dark blue or black hooded sweatshirt. The witness could not see the suspect's face due to the angle of the computer's camera; however, she glimpsed the perpetrator as they exited the room. She stated that the suspect had on sneakers with a red logo on the side. The funeral for Mr. Long will be on Monday at 2:00 p.m. at Shaw's House of Eternal Rest. The family has requested donations to the local library instead of flowers."

I blew out a deep breath of surprise. I didn't know Huey Long's family, but they must have known he liked to frequent the library. The family probably wasn't aware how much we had to fight to get our stuff back from him every month. Or what a jerk he was when he came in. I wouldn't be the one to tell them.

I got up to fix myself breakfast. I gathered eggs, mushrooms, peppers and cheese from my refrigerator and prepared an omelet. Next, two slices of cinnamon bread went into the chrome and turquoise 1950s toaster. I had discovered it in my favorite antique store. I placed it all on a vintage milk glass plate with turquoise trim and sat down at the table to enjoy it. Determined to have a good day despite the news of Huey and Carla, I sat down to eat.

After breakfast, I washed up my few dishes and got dressed to go into town to buy Dad's birthday present. I drove to Grimsley's Fine and Rare Books. I loved the bookstore. The owner, Mr. Grimsley, had called me Saturday to let me know that he had located a first edition of Ernest Hemingway's *For Whom the Bell Tolls*. Dad would be thrilled to add it to his growing collection of first editions by his favorite authors. My father was a professor of literature at the local college. He specialized in Shakespeare which is how my brother Richard, although we called him Rick, Juliet and I ended up with our names. I think I got the short end of the naming stick in the family. Nobody I knew had the name Ophelia. I didn't want to be a tragic character like my namesake. Parents should choose names without baggage.

The bell jingled as I opened the door and entered

another world. Mr. Grimsley's shop looked as I imagined a 19th-century bookstore in London would appear. The shelving was all dark cherry and large library-style tables were scattered across the hardwood floors. Beautiful Persian carpets throughout the store helped to muffle sounds.

"Hello?" I called out. I surveyed the shelves with longing. I wished my budget was as large as my wish list was long.

"Is that you, Ophelia? Give me just a minute. I'll be right out," Mr. Grimsley gave an answering shout from the back room. He offered book repair service, so his work room was in the back of the shop. I used him to repair our rare genealogy books at the library. A few minutes later, he appeared with a package wrapped in brown paper and tied up with a string.

"I have your father's book ready for you." He handed me the package. "And for you, I have something special!" Although Mr. Grimsley immigrated to the States when he was in his late twenties, he still retained his Scottish burr.

"Thank you for finding this for me. Dad will love it," I declared. I followed him to the cabinet next to the register and watched as he unlocked it. He reached up and selected a book. He handed it to me with silent reverence.

"*The Trumpeter Swan* by Temple Bailey. Oh my!" I gently opened the cover. "A first edition from 1920!" I gasped with pleasure as I looked through the pages. The illustrations were breathtaking.

"It's a gift for you, lass. It's a thank you for being

kind to my daughter when she was going through a bad spell. If not for you delivering books to her and sitting and visiting with her when she was ill." His voice trailed off as he wiped at his eyes.

"This is too much," I replied. "I was happy to visit with Catherine." Closing the book, I tried to hand it back to him.

"I won't take it back. It's a small gift for the kindness you did for me and my girl. I won't hear anything more about it." He wrapped the book up for me in brown paper. He tied it with a string and handed it to me.

"Thank you very much. I will treasure it forever." I reached out and grasped his hand in thanks. "Now let me pay you for Dad's present, and then I have to go so I can run a few errands for Mom for next week's big event."

I left the bookstore and walked up the sidewalk to For Goodness Cake. Mom had ordered a white chocolate cake with raspberry filling for the party. I promised her I would go pay for it and make sure it would be delivered on time next week. The heavenly scent of chocolate and butter cream frosting enveloped me as I opened the door of the shop. As I entered, I saw someone else was standing at the glass cases. Grace Winchester, Clint's date from the night before, was selecting a muffin. The girl behind the counter wrapped a blueberry cream cheese muffin in paper and handed it to Grace.

As she turned to leave the store, Grace almost ran into me. "Whoops! Oh, hi! Ophelia, right?"

"Yes. Hello," I responded with a chilly voice. "You're Grace. Clint's date from last night."

"Date?" She laughed and shook her head. "Don't tell my husband! No, you have it all wrong. I'm here from the state police academy to do some mandatory training. Clint was just nice enough to drag me out of my hotel room and away from vending machine food to offer me a nice dinner. He's friends with my husband, Jacob. Who also gave his blessing that I eat real food since I am eating for two." She nibbled the edges of her muffin.

"Oh really? Congratulations!" I stammered as I tried to process the fact that Clint had not been on a date with her. My heart lifted a little, but then sank as I realized Clint thought I had been on a date myself last night. Not that he cared. "How long are you here in Miller's Cove?"

"Just until Tuesday. I could have driven back home this weekend, but my husband was off on a fishing trip with his brothers. I stayed here through the weekend to do some antique shopping. Miller's Cove is a treasure chest for an antique hound like me."

"You like antiques? Me too? You should go to Jensen's Antique Emporium over on Elm Street. They give the best deals. I happen to know they have a beautiful rocking chair that would be perfect in a baby's room."

"Clint told me you know your antiques. He went on and on about how amazing your house is. I learned all about his best friend Rick's little sister, the town librarian." Grace brushed some crumbs that had fallen on the front of her blouse.

"Really? He talked about me?" I couldn't stop the huge grin that spread across my face. "I mean, I'm glad he likes my house. It took a lot of time to decorate it just right." I tried playing it cool. Inside I felt like a middle school kid receiving her first invitation to the dance.

"Yep. Well, I've got to go. Lots of shops to visit today. It was nice seeing you again." Grace gave me a quick wave goodbye and headed out of the shop. Still smiling like a cat who found the hidden catnip stash, I headed to the counter to pay for the cake.

CHAPTER ELEVEN

The following week was busy at the library as we had our annual Fall Book Sale to raise money for new programs. Local author and semi-celebrity, Joanna Franklin, came on Wednesday to give a talk on how she became a writer. That evening after I had closed up the library, I swung by Odd Couple's to grab a bite to eat. My cupboards at home were bare, and I was too tired to go to Abe's Market.

Odd Couple's Diner was a step back in time. It was an authentic 1950s diner that the current owner had vowed to keep intact when he inherited it from his grandparents. The owners, Seth Hansen and his wife Stephanie, were a young couple in their late twenties. Seth had served four years in the Coast Guard. When he came home, he had gone to work with his grandparents. Last year, Ida and Melba Hansen started spending their winters in Florida. They handed the keys to the diner over to Seth as an early inheritance and headed south. The diner served burgers and sandwiches named after 1950s actors, musicians and such. I settled on Bleu Suede Shoes - a charbroiled burger smothered with bleu cheese and served on a grilled Kaiser bun. Thick cut fries topped it all off. I would have to walk ten miles to burn off the calories, but it was well worth it.

"Care if I join you?" Clint stood next to my booth with his hat in his hands.

"Sure." I looked up at him and my cheeks flushed a

little. "I've ordered, but you can probably catch Stephanie before she gives it to the kitchen."

Stephanie walked over to the booth to set down my root beer. "Hi there, Clint. What can I get for you?"

"I think I'll get the Chubby Checker. Can you put an extra slice of pepper jack cheese on it for me and hold the onions? And a glass of tea, please." Clint set his hat on the seat next to him and leaned back. "What a day! The whole town is going nuts with Huey Long's murder. I've had about a hundred calls from people saying they saw someone in their backyard and can we come check it out. Everyone's on edge and people are scared. I haven't had a bite to eat all day."

"It's a small town. People are nervous that someone they go to church with might be a killer. Any word on how Carla died? I read about her odd death in the newspaper." As I sipped my root beer through my straw, I looked up at him and fluttered my eyelashes. I hoped I looked like a young ingénue from a 1950s classic film.

"Do you have something caught in your eye?" Clint asked ruining my attempt at channeling Marilyn Monroe. "No. It'll take at least a few days to get the toxicology reports back from Carla's autopsy. Chris is a mess. He and Carla had been going through some tough times with their marriage, but the week before they had started marriage counseling. They were even talking about starting a family. Now, Carla is dead, and no one knows how or why. Poor guy."

"It's sad. I'll be honest with you. Carla has never been very nice, but I certainly didn't want her dead. I feel horrible about Huey, too. He was always grabbing at me and making lewd comments. Now I realize he was a lonely little man who didn't understand he came across as creepy rather than suave." I hung my head as a wave of guilt for hating them both washed over me. Stephanie came with our plates of food. We both were silent while we savored our burgers.

"I'm so hungry right now I could eat ten of these," Clint said after taking another bite of his burger. "Can we talk about something else besides death, please? I know I've about had my fill of it after the past few days."

"Well, I can tell you all about how I worried I had silverfish in my genealogy collection." I grinned across the table at him. "In the library world, that's big time crime."

"How did you solve the case, Miss Marple?" Clint played along.

"It turns out it was a piece of thread from a bookmark that Mrs. Grimes saw. Her eyesight is getting as bad as her hearing. Poor thing." I took a bite of my fries. I grabbed the salt shaker and shook some onto my plate.

"You are a true crime stopper," Clint chuckled. "Mrs. Grimes was one of my calls from today. I had to go through every room in her house looking for a possible burglar. It turns out that the noise she heard outside was a stray cat going through her garbage."

We ate in companionable silence after that. When I had finished the last French fry, I sat back in my seat to find Clint watching me. "What?" I asked. "Do I have something on my face?" I wiped my mouth with my napkin.

"No. I was just sitting here contemplating how nice it is to spend time with you. I'm comfortable with you. Most girls feel the need to chatter about nothing because they have to fill the silence. You don't ever do that. I like it. You missed a spot of bleu cheese on your cheek though." He reached across the table and wiped the corner of my mouth with his napkin. "Much better. Don't want anything to mess up that pretty face."

"You think I'm pretty?" I became shy and uncomfortable. I squirmed a little in my seat.

"Ophelia Jefferson, I don't think it. I *know* you're beautiful," Clint said with a soft voice as he took my hand.

"Thanks. I think you're beautiful, too." I turned beet red and stammered, "I mean handsome."

Clint laughed. "I'm good with handsome. I'd better get back to work, Phee. If I don't see you before then, I'll see you at your dad's big birthday bash." He stood up, grabbed the check off the table and went to the register. I loved to watch that man walk. I leaned back and gave a sigh of contentment. Deciding to walk on the wild side, I ordered a slice of Sugar and Spice and Everything Nice Apple Pie. Life's too short to pass up dessert.

CHAPTER TWELVE

The rest of the week passed quickly. Before I knew it, it was Sunday evening and the day of my dad's party. I took my time getting ready for the night's festivities. Mom had called earlier and advised me that quite a few more people than originally planned were coming to celebrate Dad's big 6-0. Because the weather was warm for fall, she decided to have it on the patio overlooking the cove. I spent the afternoon running around town purchasing lights to hang across the back yard and citronella candles to keep the mosquitoes at bay. After I dropped off the cake and the lights to Mom, I hurried home to get showered and dressed.

I had purchased an emerald green silk halter dress and a beautiful ombre shawl in complementary shades. I coiled my long, curly hair up into a chignon secured with a silver hair comb. I added a silver cuff bracelet with a Celtic design and dainty silver hoop earrings with green jade stones. A swipe of silvery shadow across my lids and a hint of liner and black mascara completed my makeup. For a final touch, I applied a soft petal pink lip stain. Looking in my vanity mirror, I felt pleased with the result. Clint had mentioned seeing me at the party. I decided tonight he would see me as Ophelia Jefferson, gorgeous woman of intrigue, and not as Flea, Rick Jefferson's little sister. I slipped my newly polished toes into a pair of green and silver sandals with a kitten heel and headed out the door.

As I drove up to my parent's house, I saw that the

caterer's van was already there. I walked around the side of the house and into my parent's backyard. Mom and the caterers had done a marvelous job transforming the patio. Several long tables set around the yard would accommodate the added party-goers. The lights crisscrossed the patio and lanterns of varying shades hung from the trees. She had created centerpieces using fall leaves and candles floating in water-filled, light green glass bowls. The caterers were busy grilling and setting out the side dishes. I spotted Mom fussing with the cake next to the gift table. I walked over to her and placed my Dad's present on the table.

"Hi, darling! What do you think?" Mom gestured to the patio.

"It looks magical. You've done an amazing job with everything. Dad will love it. Where is he?" I looked around but didn't see him.

"He's hiding out in the den since he says I drive him crazy with all of my fussing." Mom laughed. My parents still acted like teenagers in love. They had met at the university when my dad was finishing his PhD in English and my mom was studying for her Master's degree in art history. Dad said it was love at first sight when he spotted my mom sitting in the Quad. He said she sat there quietly drawing underneath a tree and was oblivious to everyone and everything around her. He had been playing Frisbee with his friends and had "accidentally" let it land in the grass at her feet. They have been together ever since then.

"Do you need my help with anything?" I offered as I looked around to see what else needed to be done.

"No, but thank you. You go on in and visit with your dad," Mom replied. "The band will be here in a few minutes, and I need to get them situated and ready to play before the guests arrive. Everyone should be here in the next half hour."

"Alright. If you're sure, I'll go hang out with Dad." I turned and headed through the French doors and went to go find Dad in his "man cave" as Juliet and I called it. I spotted him sleeping on his leather couch. He had fallen asleep with a book on his chest, and he was gently snoring. Our Irish Setter, Hamlet, was asleep on the floor next to him. I tiptoed out and shut the door. I went to hang out in the kitchen and stay out of my mother's way. She was tougher than a drill sergeant at boot camp for hosting parties. My brother, sister and I were smart soldiers and kept our heads down and ran for cover when party planning was in full swing.

I poured myself a glass of lemonade and sat on a kitchen stool. I watched through the window as Mom directed the band to their designated spots. It would be great to have everyone here. Dad's brother, Uncle Paul, was driving up to surprise Dad. Uncle Paul retired from the Marine Corps after serving twenty years as a sniper. He lived in a remote cabin two hours from Miller's Cove and didn't venture out too often.

"Hey there, PheePhee." Rick walked into the kitchen followed by his pregnant wife, Carrie. "Supposedly you are doing a little B & E. Interesting career move. How's that working for you?"

Carrie swatted him. "Rick, leave your sister alone. I'm sure she is upset enough about what happened without you picking on her. Sheesh! What are you?

61

twelve?"

"Today I'm feeling a young ten," Rick joked. He leaned over, kissed Carrie and rubbed her protruding belly. "Don't worry R.J. and C.J. I won't let your bad Aunt PheePhee lead you into a life of crime."

"Ha ha. My family is full of comedians. I assume Clint told you since it's supposed to be top secret." I glared at him in mock anger. "Quit calling me PheePhee. I am not a French Poodle."

"Yep." Rick opened the refrigerator and pulled out a beer. He twisted the top off and gave me a stern look. "You should be glad it was Clint that took the call. Otherwise you might be in the big house. We'd have to change your name to Hoosegow Honey."

"Whatever. Just promise you won't tell Mom and Dad. Especially not tonight!" I admonished him. Rick might be older than me, but most of the time, I felt like his big sister.

"Hmmm…My silence can be bought." Rick stroked his upper lip as if he were an evil villain with a handlebar mustache.

"Enough you two! At least you both give me experience on dealing with bickering siblings." Carrie laughed and rubbed her stomach.

"How are the twins? And how are you? You look marvelous. I can't believe it's already been seven months!" I adored my sister-in-law. She would be a phenomenal mother and her gentle nature was a good balance to Rick's hyperactive, comedic personality.

"I'm okay. Just tired most days," Carrie replied.

"I'm glad I could start my maternity leave early. I don't think I could take teaching a room full of active kindergartners right now. Rick swears all I do is eat and sleep. The doctor said that he may put me on bed rest for the final month. As exhausted as I am, I am looking forward to it!"

"I will be happy to supply you with all the books, movies and chocolate bonbons your heart could desire. So excited to meet my niece and nephew!" I looked forward to being an aunt. Although not ready for children yet, I liked to imagine a future family. I wondered if they might inherit their father's green eyes.

"Phee?" Startled, I realized I had been daydreaming and Carrie was talking. "You were a million miles away. What were you thinking?"

"Oh, nothing. Planning what to get for the babies' first Christmas," I fibbed. I heard the front door open and Juliet's voice. She walked in the kitchen and behind her stood Wade. I did a quick double take. Where was his wheelchair?

"What? What's going on here? Wade? Are you standing?" The shock made me stumble over my words.

"Yup!" Wade leaned over and tapped where his calves used to be before the IED. "I'm bionic, baby!" A wide grin split his face.

"Oh my gosh! When? Where? How? Hey! How did you keep this a secret from me?" I demanded.

"Whoa! When? Oh, about 5 months ago, but I kept my physical therapy a secret because what if I couldn't do it? I've been visiting the V.A. hospital over in

Burlington on my days off. And, Phee, you're so easy to keep secrets from. No offense, but you live in your own little world sometimes," Wade said.

I sniffled a little. I walked over and gave him a huge hug. "I'm happy for you, my friend. I even forgive you for keeping it a secret from me." I released him and looked at my sister. Then I looked down and realized that she and Wade were holding hands. Juliet must have been the "hot date" from the other day.

"And?" I hinted and looked at their clasped hands.

"And I ran into Wade when I was teaching yoga over at the V.A. I do a modified routine for people in chairs or who aren't as mobile. Wade showed up for one of my classes. We had coffee afterwards and one thing led to another..." Juliet shrugged her shoulders.

"I can't believe you kept it a secret from me!" I needed to pay attention because I was obviously clueless to things happening around me.

"It was my decision to keep it a secret," Wade replied. "Juliet wanted to tell you after the first date, but I told her I wanted to wait. You are my boss. It might make things a little weird between us."

"I forgive you, but only because I am so happy that one, you are walking, and two, you are dating my flaky sister!" I teased them.

"Hey now! I am not a flake. I operate on another plane of existence than the rest of you unenlightened people," Juliet protested.

Just then, Dad walked into the kitchen. His red hair was a mess after his nap. It stuck out at angles that must have confounded gravity and a comb.

"Greetings and salutations, progeny!" Dad yawned "Where's your mom?"

"Hello, father dearest!" Rick, Juliet and I chimed in unison. We burst out laughing. Carrie and Wade looked at us, then at each other and shook their heads.

"Mom's out on the patio directing the band," I informed him. "But she will murder you if you go out there without straightening up a little after your nap. You'd better hurry because I see that Sheriff Dawes and Sheila have already arrived. We'd better head out."

"Tell your mother I will be out in a second. I need to make myself gorgeous for my fans." Dad wiggled his eyebrows and pretended to pat his hair like a Hollywood starlet from the 1950s. He turned and headed down the hallway.

The rest of us walked outside to greet the arriving guests.

CHAPTER THIRTEEN

The party was going full swing. Mom and Dad were dancing to the Bee Gees. Rick, Juliet and I pretended not to be mortified by Dad's John Travolta arm. Everyone seemed to have fun. Grant arrived with his mom. Shari looked haunted compared to the last time I saw her. Her husband's death must be taking a toll on her. I decided to make a point to go visit her more often.

"Shari! I am glad you could come this evening. You must be happy to have Grant home with you," I said.

"I'm thrilled, Phee. You and Grant should stop by next Saturday. I will make you my famous fried chicken. I remember how much you loved it as a girl." Shari was a soft-spoken woman, and I had to lean in to hear her over the band.

"I'd love to come visit. I'm happy as a kitten in cream to have my best movie buddy back home." I bumped Grant with my hip and he smiled.

"Wait a minute there, Phee. You can't just use me for my outstanding taste in Whoppers, popcorn and Jujubes," Grant joked. "Mom, let me get you settled at the table. I will show Phee my show stopping dance moves. Fred Astaire has nothing on me." Grant did a little shuffle with his feet. He tucked his arm around his mother and led her towards a corner table.

"I can't believe how fragile his mother looks. She has always looked strong and tan from all of her gardening, but now she seems faded," I remarked to Juliet. "I loved going to her house after school because she was always so much fun. She made the best root beer floats for Grant and me. Mr. Davis' death took its toll on her. She's aged twenty years overnight."

"Sad," Juliet said shaking her head. "I bet you're glad to have Grant back. He has had a huge crush on you for forever."

"You're wrong," I replied. "He and I tried to go on a date once in high school. We both decided that our friendship was too important to risk. I'm sad we lost touch."

"I'm telling you that I know when a guy is interested in a girl as more than friends. Grant may say he is okay with just being friends, but his body language says something else." Juliet gave me a knowing look.

Grant walked over, bowed and held out his hand. "M'lady. Might I be honored with the pleasure of your company on the dance floor?"

"Why, sir, I'd be delighted!" I said in my best Scarlett O'Hara voice. I took his hand. As we walked to the patio where the other couples were dancing, the band played Doris Day's *Again*. Grant swung me into his arms and we swayed back and forth.

"I remembered this was one of your favorite songs," Grant said softly. His hand tightened on my lower back as he guided me around the small dance area.

"You have a great memory, my friend," I said lightly. I loved Grant but as a friend. Perhaps Juliet was right, but I hoped not. I didn't want things to be uncomfortable between us.

"We could be more than friends," Grant said huskily. "I mean, we're no longer teenagers, Phee."

"Can I cut in?" A deep voice asked from behind me. Clint was standing off to the side. He held his hand out to me.

"Sure. Why not?" Grant responded with a voice barely short of a snarl. He handed me over to Clint and stalked away.

"Lover's quarrel?" Clint raised an eyebrow and looked down at me. He pulled me closer to him.

I sighed. "No. I'm realizing he wants something more than I am willing to give. It's complicated." I looked up at him and noticed the dark circles under his eyes. "You look exhausted."

"I am, but I couldn't disappoint your parents. Besides, I needed to dance with the prettiest girl in the room." His eyes swept over me and paused at the plunging neckline of my dress. "You're beautiful, Ophelia."

"Thank you," I whispered and ducked my head. I moved a little closer to him. We danced under the moon and the world faded away. In my mind, it was only the two of us out there on the patio. All too soon, the music ended, and the band played ABBA's *Mama Mia*. My mother and Sheila Dawes sang and dance in a spoof of the musical and the moment was over.

Clint walked me over to the makeshift Tiki bar that my Mom had set up for the party. He ordered a Cosmopolitan for me and a tap beer for himself. We walked over to the corner farthest from the band. Clint yawned.

"Late night?" I asked, hoping it was from work and not from a new girlfriend.

"Yes." He took a long draw from his beer. "I spent the night over at Chris Karsen's. Phee, I might as well tell you now since there will be a press release in the morning. Carla was murdered. The autopsy results came back and I had to break the news to Chris. He took it hard."

I gave out a shocked gasp, "How?"

"At first, they thought it was severe food poisoning. She and Chris had gone to the benefit breakfast over at the fire department Saturday morning. She was the only one who became ill so that helped to rule out food poisoning. Based upon her symptoms and the contents of her stomach, she ingested some kind of poisonous mushroom. It had to have been intentional. With half the town at the breakfast, it will be next to impossible to narrow down the suspects at this point. Heck! Your brother was there, Grant and his mom, Cincinnati, your sister and Wade were all there helping out and eating. It is going to take me a week to get all the witness statements." Clint groaned and ran his fingers through his dark hair in a frustration.

"This is awful. I feel horrible because I argued with both Carla and Huey last week. I should have been nicer." I was lower than a worm. First, I had gotten angry with Huey. Next, I insulted Carla. They weren't nice, but I should have been the better person.

"I know you said you didn't like Carla, but I didn't

realize you argued with her. What about?" Clint took another sip of beer.

"It's no big secret. She wanted to tear down the library and build a new recreation center with a gym and pool. She had already approached the rest of the town council. Carla was browbeating me to accept defeat and skulk away with my tail between my legs. I refused and told her that just because she couldn't read, didn't mean the rest of the town was illiterate." I grimaced at how harsh I had been. "I guess I wasn't very nice."

"Who else knew about your argument with her?" Clint asked.

"Anyone who attended the town council meeting. Anyone who talked about it afterwards would know, too. Cincinnati was with me when she accosted me on the sidewalk the other day. Everybody in town knew that there was no love lost between the two of us. You had already graduated, but she made my life a living hell in high school and hasn't let up since. She is the reason Grant and I became friends. He came to my rescue after she played a joke on me." I shook my head. "Sorry. I'm not much help, am I? I wish I could narrow it down for you."

"What about you and Huey Long? Who knew about your problems with him?" Clint asked.

"Many people. I wasn't quiet when I yelled at him after he made some nasty comment about how he had a library card and would like to check me out. This was after he pinched me on my butt." I shuddered as I remembered the hungry look in Huey Long's eyes as he leered at me. Huey had a habit of looking at me like I was a steak and egg breakfast, and he was a starving man.

"Hmm..." Clint frowned. "Well, this isn't common knowledge, so you need to keep this to yourself. Huey was the prime suspect in a series of rare book and map thefts in the area. It appears he was going to the university libraries throughout the state and somehow cutting illustrations and maps from rare texts and selling them overseas. Your buddy, Grant, was Huey's defense attorney. He was probably casing the library's rare books and used his obnoxious behavior to make sure you wouldn't bother him."

"Holy Toledo! I didn't like the man because he was always really slimy to me. He made me think he was undressing me every time he looked at me. I never imagined he was a thief, too." It dismayed me to realize he may have stolen from the town library.

Clint placed an arm around my shoulder. "Phee, it looks like someone is killing off anyone who mistreats you." Shocked, I looked up at him and saw he was serious.

CHAPTER FOURTEEN

"What are you two kids doing holed up in the corner?" Sheriff Jaime Dawes sidled over to us. A short man, he had his Hispanic mother's dark eyes and hair and his father's Irish features. The swagger was all his own.

"Sir," Clint nodded his head respectfully to his boss. "This isn't the best time but after talking to Phee, I think I found one thing that Huey Long and Carla Karsen had in common."

"What's that?" Sheriff Dawes inquired.

"Her." Clint pointed at me. "Both victims had conflicts with her in the days leading up to their murders. Phee had an alibi for Mr. Long's murder, so she's in the clear, but it might be someone close to her."

"I was at work Saturday when Carla was poisoned," I volunteered.

"That's good to know," Sheriff Dawes said with a hint of too much happiness for the topic of murder. I wondered how many beers he and my father had already drank together. "Come into the office tomorrow and we'll talk about this more, but tonight...tonight we are here to celebrate my friend's birthday." He raised his beer in a toast and began a tango across the patio to his wife, Sheila.

"He's a little toasted already." I smiled. "Can we please forget about all this death and nastiness for tonight?"

"I'm sorry," Clint frowned. "I wasn't thinking. We can. I have a beautiful woman standing next to me, and all I can do is talk about work. Let's go get something to eat." He held out his arm. Not hesitating for a second, I reached out and took it. We walked across to where the caterers had set up the food. Clint handed me a plate and took one for him. We filled our plates and then looked around for some empty chairs. We spotted two chairs next to Grant and his mother and wound our way through the dancers to sit next to them.

"Thought I had lost you for the evening," Grant pouted like a sullen toddler when we sat down.

"No. Clint just had some news to share with me." I felt annoyed with Grant's possessive attitude.

"This has turned out to be a wonderful evening," Shari chimed in.

"It has," I agreed. "Clint, you were a senior when Grant and I were freshmen in high school. I doubt you and Grant knew each other too well." I hoped my pitiful attempt at small talk would ease some of the tension. Grant and I would have a talk about our friendship. He was becoming too possessive and acting like a boyfriend instead of a friend.

"You were a first class debate team captain if I recall." Clint helped me to steer the conversation back to neutral ground.

"Thanks. I think I knew even then I wanted to be a courtroom attorney." Grant puffed up a little. "Phee, did you hear about Carla Karsen?"

"Yes," I said. "Terrible way to die. She and I were definitely not friends, but I didn't want her dead."

"Well, I don't know what I feel about it. I saw her Saturday morning at the benefit breakfast at the fire department," Grant said. "She knows you and I are friends, Phee, yet she went on and on about how you were standing in the way of progress."

"Well, I hope you defended me!" I tried to joke even though it wasn't a joking matter. "Did you know Huey Long?" I tried to be nonchalant, but Clint rolled his eyes.

"I did," Grant did not continue.

"How did you know him?" I persisted. If looks could kill, Clint left me drawn and quartered on the floor. I ignored him. It wasn't him inciting violence and death. Clint needed information, and I was helping him get it. He should be grateful.

"I guess it wouldn't hurt to say anything now that he's dead. Huey was a client at my firm. But I can't give you any more details than that or I would violate attorney client privilege," Grant offered. "I will say he had a crush on you, Phee."

"What the heck?!" I exclaimed. "No way! He was always such a creep to me."

"That's surprising. He commented he thought you were "pretty nice looking for a nerd." I think those were his words. I have to say he was right. You look amazing tonight," Grant said.

"Thank you," I accepted his compliment. "But you say that only because you've seen me after chugging

Boone's Farm and upchucking behind the bleachers after a football game. Anything would be an improvement over that!"

"You kids!" Shari laughed. "I remember that night because your mom called me to make sure I grounded Grant for as long as she grounded you. Now the two of you are all grown up and ready to settle down and start a family."

An awkward silence filled the air after Shari's comment. I realized Clint was left out of the conversation. He was already off at police academy when Grant and I were up to our teenage shenanigans. Changing the topic, I said, "I hope my dad's having fun with this evening. My mom went a little crazy getting everything ready."

"It looks like they are having a great time." Clint nodded in my parent's direction. They were slow dancing to Aerosmith's *Angel*.

My Uncle Paul walked up to our table and pulled up a chair. After leaving the Marines, he had given up the high and tight and morphed into a full mountain man. He had a bushy gray beard and wore flannel on a daily basis. His footwear would never change though. He still wore his combat boots no matter what the occasion. He probably wanted to be buried in them.

"There's my girl!" Uncle Paul boomed. "I've been looking all over the place for you. Have you been hiding all night?"

"I've been right here," I stood up and gave him a hug. "How are you, Uncle Paul? Any new projects up there on the mountain?"

"I'm good. I'm good." He nodded. "I've been studying up on wild foods. I've been learning how to identify mushrooms and other edibles. Morels, fiddleheads, all sorts of things. In fact, I met a fellow just the other day out in the woods who said he knew you, Phee."

"Me? Who was it?" I asked.

"He was a long-haired hippie that went to school with you and Grant. I think his name was Duane. Real interesting fella. He could identify every mushroom in the forest. He pointed out which ones were poisonous and which were okay to eat. I don't know. I might just stick with the store-bought ones. Seems safer that way." Uncle Paul declared.

"Duane and I were good friends in school," Grant offered. "He spent most of his free time outdoors. I loved going out with him and learning about the different plants and animals. You're right, Paul. He could tell you all about mushrooms. I remember him telling me about one called the 'avenging angel' or something like that."

"I think he called it the 'destroying angel'. The way he tells it, it can kill you in less than a day. It causes bad crap to happen. You hallucinate, become delirious and sick as hell to your stomach before you up and meet the big general in the sky. And that is why I think I will buy my mushrooms from the local grocer. Like my sainted mother always said, it is better to be safe than sorry," Uncle Paul finished emphatically and took a draw from his bottle of beer.

Clint had been listening closely during the

discussion. "What's the name of this friend of yours? He's an expert on mushrooms?"

"He's younger than you, so you might not remember him. Duane Phillips. We were all classmates. He comes in the library all the time. He just did a presentation there two weeks ago for the public," I said. I wondered why Clint was asking about Duane. Then it hit me. Carla was poisoned by a mushroom.

"I'd like to meet this friend of yours," Clint said. "I think I need to ask him a few questions about poisonous mushrooms."

CHAPTER FIFTEEN

The party was winding down around ten o'clock. My dad was over the moon at my present. The band was closing down the evening with a series of Journey tunes. I took a break from the crowd and walked to the beach. I picked my way down the pebble path and found my favorite fallen oak tree near the shore and took a seat. I loved sitting down here and listening to the sound of the water lapping at the rocks. In the distance, the hoot of a horned owl sounded from the tree-lined shore. The warm September breeze nudged a wisp of hair loose from my chignon.

"Is this seat taken?" Clint took a seat next to me. We sat quietly together for a few minutes while savoring the beautiful evening. The music drifted on the night air, and I could hear the band singing *Faithfully*. Clint stood up and held out his hand. I took it, and he pulled me into his arms. We began a slow dance in the sand. I rested my head on his chest. He smelled of leather, wood smoke and a hint of citrus. I inhaled deeply as I tried to memorize the scent of him. As the last notes of the song wound down, Clint placed a finger on my chin, bent down and softly kissed me. I leaned into him and when our lips parted, I felt his arm tighten around my waist. He gazed down at me.

"Ophelia," Clint whispered. "What are you doing to me?"

"I don't know," I whispered back to him. "I just

know that I'd like for you to kiss me again." Clint gave a low throaty chuckle and leaned down to kiss me. A sudden snap echoing from the woods startled us apart. Clint's hand went to his hip where he normally had his gun, but he realized it wasn't there. He held his finger up to his lips and moved towards the tree line. There was a rustle in the leaves.

"Hey guys! We've been looking everywhere for you!" Juliet's voice called out from the path above us. I looked up and saw Rick stumbling down the path with Juliet. Both of them were laughing. Clint stopped his movement towards the woods. He took one last glance, shook his head and turned back towards me.

"What are you doing down here, PheePhee?" Rick asked.

"Oh, I was just down here getting some fresh air and taking a break from the music. Clint came down here to get me and bring me back to the party," I said smoothly. "We'd better head back up there. I am sure people are getting ready to head home." I walked up the path towards the patio. My heel caught on a stone and as I stumbled, I felt strong arms grasp me.

"You'd better hold on to my arm before you fall." Clint offered. I felt a small ripple of happiness as I walked next to him arm in arm.

"If she didn't wear those girly girl shoes, she wouldn't need help!" Rick grumbled. "But I guess she'd look pretty silly in that dress and a pair of combat boots." I laughed at the idea of Super Librarian in her bedazzled mask and combat boots.

As we crested the slight rise leading to the patio, I

saw that the party was breaking up. We stopped and chatted with a few folks who were getting ready to leave. A few moments later, I spotted Grant at the edge of the patio near the woods. He strode up to me. I caught an angry, possessive look in his eyes I'd never seen.

"I wondered where you had disappeared to and I guess now I know." He gave a pointed stare at my hand resting on Clint's arms. I dropped my hand away.

"Phee stumbled on the rocks down at the beach because of her heels. I am sure you wouldn't want her to fall and hurt herself. Don't worry. I brought her back safe and sound to you," Clint said sardonically as he stepped away from me. I looked from Grant to Clint and back again. At first, confusion and hurt rolled through me at Clint's sudden change, but then I got pissed at both he and Grant's macho posturing.

"I am so glad I have two such manly men to take care of little ole' me." I glowered at them both. "I don't need either one of you treating me like I am a kid or a possession." I stamped my foot, turned and walked away from both of them to where my parents were saying goodbye to their departing guests.

"Great party, Mom. If you don't need me this evening, I'm bushed so I think I'll head home. I'll be stop by early in the morning to pick up the tables in Velma and return them on my lunch break to the party store." I hugged them both. "Happy birthday, Dad. I love you."

"I love you, too, honey. Be careful heading home," Dad said. I walked through the house and out the front door towards Velma, my faithful ride. I reached over to fasten my seat belt. As I turned back, a shadow fell across my window. I looked over to see Grant outside my driver's side window with his hand raised to knock on it. I rolled my window down.

"What do you want, Grant? It's been a long night. I'm tired and I'm not in the mood for testosterone wars." I frowned at him. I didn't recognize or like this new Grant who played the possessive card.

"I just wanted to apologize," Grant said, a sheepish look on his face. "I acted like an ass. I can only blame it on the fact that I've come back home and my best friend is no longer a hippie chick with a mouth full of metal and her nose always buried in a book. She's replaced by a very attractive chick with her nose still buried in a book. Forgive me?"

"I suppose," I said grudgingly. Hearing the sincerity in his voice, I gave up trying to be angry with him and smiled.

"Good. I've got to get mom home. It is way past her normal bedtime, but it was good for her to get out of the house. She even danced with Sheriff Dawes," Grant said.

"I'll talk to you later. Glad your mom had fun. Call me later this week and we'll grab a sandwich or something." I rolled up the window and started the van. Once I got home, I pulled a cotton nightgown over my head and fell into bed. I was asleep before I could count ten sheep.

CHAPTER SIXTEEN

At eight o'clock the next morning, I drove to my parents' house to pick up the tables. Dad was in his striped pajamas and ratty flannel robe that Mom swore she would use to scrub the floors but never did. He slipped on some tennis shoes and helped me pick up the tables and carry them from the garage. We loaded them into the back of Velma. My mom was still in bed recovering from the night before.

"I noticed you and Clint seemed to have something going on between you. Anything you want to share with your old man?" Dad hoisted the final table into the van and shut the door.

"Not sure there is anything to share at this point," I said. I leaned against the bumper.

"Ophelia, I hate to tell you this, but you wear your heart on your sleeve for that boy. You always have." Dad sat down on the bumper next to me.

"I don't think Rick would be too thrilled with Clint dating his little sister." I plucked at the hem of my cardigan.

"Rick is a big boy and needs to realize his baby sister has grown up. Besides, he and Carrie will be so tired when the twins are born that he won't have the energy to argue about it," Dad joked. He leaned over and kissed me on my forehead. "Follow what's in your heart and you'll be just fine."

I stood up and gave him a hug. "Thanks, Dad. I better get going if I don't want to be late for work." I hopped in Velma, fired her up and headed down the driveway. I rolled down the window and gave my dad a little wave as I turned out onto the street.

I arrived at work with a few minutes to spare before opening. Fortunately, Wade was already there. His years in the military guaranteed he would be on time. He had emptied the book drop and was busy checking in the books. He was back in the wheelchair.

"Howdy, boss!" Wade said cheerfully. He didn't appear the least bit tired despite our late evening. "Are we all good?"

I raised an eyebrow at him. "With you and Juliet? Definitely. Let me know if she misbehaves. I'll put Ex-Lax in her brownies like I did when we were kids. She was mad at me for a month after that."

Laughing, Wade said, "Will do. Remind me not to get on your bad side."

"What's up with the wheels?" I pointed to his chair.

"I'm still getting used to wearing my new legs. My knees get sore where they attach, and last night put a strain on them. It was well worth it to get up and dance to one song." Wade rolled over to the cart and placed the books in Dewey Decimal order.

It was time to open, so I left him to his work. I unlocked the doors, and we started our day. I did story time with the local preschool on Mondays. The children lined up outside ready to march in when their teacher gave the okay. One by one, they trooped in and settled into a semi-circle in front of the Mother Goose chair in the children's zone. Sitting on the chair, I opened a picture book and read the story. We giggled and laughed our way through a series of silly rhymes.

At noon, I told Wade I'd be back in an hour and headed downtown to Party Peeps to return the tables. Once I finished, I headed across the street to Odd Couple's Diner to grab a cup of coffee and a tuna fish sandwich. I picked up an extra cup of coffee for Wade and headed back to work. I parked Velma in the lot next to the library and headed inside. It was a chore to balance the two hot cups of coffee and the bag with my sandwich and chips. The door to the library opened, and Duane Phillips stepped out.

"Let me help you with that, Phee." Duane hurried to grab one of the cups in my hand. We walked into the library together. I handed Wade his coffee.

"Thanks, Duane. Awesome job on the nature program the other week. We were talking about you last night as a matter of fact." I set my bag and coffee on top of my desk.

"All good things, I hope!" Duane tugged his slouched hat off his dreadlocks. A slight hint of patchouli hung in the surrounding air.

"You know Deputy Clint Mason? He was at my parent's party last night. He was really interested when he heard you were a mushroom hunter," I informed him. "You'll probably be getting a visit from him some time soon."

"You don't say," Duane said nervously. "Thanks. I'll keep an eye out for him. I'd better hit the road. I've got some, uh, business to take care of." He sprinted out of the building.

"Well, that was a little odd," I remarked to Wade. "Duane just acted weird when I mentioned Clint wanted to talk to him about mushroom hunting."

Wade let out a large guffaw. "No wonder he's nervous. I don't think he wants the police visiting his trailer in the woods."

"Why not?" I asked.

Wade laughed harder. "Never mind. If you don't know, I won't explain."

Shaking my head in confusion, I unwrapped my sandwich and took a bite. I thought about what Clint had said last night regarding the murders. I argued with both Huey and Carla within days of their deaths. It was probably just a coincidence. Miller's Cove was a small village of less than five thousand people. Other people knew both of them. If I considered how abrasive they both were, it was possible someone else argued with them. I took another bite of my sandwich as I puzzled over who else disliked Karla and Huey as much as I did. I picked up the phone and dialed Grant's office number.

"Grant Davis," Grant answered.

"Ooh, you sound so grown up," I joked.

"Phee! What a great party last night. Sorry things got a little weird between us," he said.

"No worries. Hey, the reason I called is that Clint mentioned something and since you're an attorney, I wanted to get your opinion. Both Huey Long and Carla Karsen argued with me shortly before they died. Clint suggested the thing they both had in common was me. I'm going by the sheriff's office later this afternoon to give Sheriff Dawes more information. What do you think? Should I be worried?" I took a sip of my coffee while I waited for his answer.

"I wouldn't worry about it too much, Phee. I am sure they both interacted with lots of people. The fact that you argued with them both is probably just a coincidence," Grant reassured me. "Do you want me to come with you to the sheriff's office? I have an open hour around four o'clock this afternoon."

"Thanks, but no. I should be fine. It's made me a little uneasy. Listen. I'll call you after I get done. We can grab dinner and rehash it," I suggested.

"Sounds good, Phee. I've got to go. I have a client waiting for me. Call me when you're done." He disconnected the line.

I spent the next hour paying bills and ordering books. At three o'clock, I got up, slipped on a cardigan and walked to the sheriff's office. I told the receptionist my name and that I was here to talk to Sheriff Dawes.

"Is he expecting you?" She was polishing her nails and looked annoyed that I interrupted her grooming session. She probably wasn't used to visitors. Miller's Cove was a small town with little crime in the winter beyond a few small busts for illegal possession of pot and the occasional domestic disturbance. In the summer when the lake cabins rented out, the crime picked up. We were a safe community. These two murders were the first in over one hundred years.

"He asked me to stop by this afternoon. If he's not free, I can come back later." I waited while she buzzed the sheriff.

"He said to go on back. First door on the right." She pointed me toward his office. The heels of my Mary Janes clicked loudly on the tiles as I walked down the hall. I knocked on the door jamb outside Sheriff Dawes' office.

"Come on in, Ophelia. Great time at your folks' place last night. Have a seat." He indicated a sturdy, uncomfortable looking chair in front of his large oak desk. Files were stacked willy nilly on it. It looked as if the slightest breeze would set everything tumbling. I sat down, crossed my ankles and waited. "I wanted to follow up with you on what Clint mentioned last night."

"About that Sheriff Dawes..." I began.

"Call me Jaime. You're no longer a little girl with pigtails." He gave me a fatherly smile.

"Ok. Jaime. I've been thinking about what Clint said about me being what Huey and Carla had in common. I mean, them both arguing with me," I explained.

"Don't worry, Ophelia. I verified your whereabouts at the time of death for both victims. You were at dinner with Juliet when Huey died and at work when Carla consumed the poisoned mushrooms. To be honest, I think the fact you argued with the two of them is not that significant. I'll ask around, but between you and me, neither one was popular with other folks. The only reason Carla was on the town council was because no one ran against her." Jaime leaned back in his chair. "Listen, I'll call you if anything pans out with this idea of Clint's, but I wouldn't worry about it too much." He stood up. I followed suit and headed towards the door.

"Thanks, Jaime. You've made me feel a little better. I suppose the guilt will make me be kinder to difficult people in the future." I walked down the hallway. The sheriff followed behind me.

"Don't fret too much about it. Tell your folks thanks again for a great party. Thanks for stopping by." He turned and went back to his office. I left the building and headed back to the library.

CHAPTER SEVENTEEN

Once home from work, I remembered I had forgotten to call Grant. I dialed his cell phone. When I got no answer, I left him a quick message telling him everything went fine at the sheriff's office. I let him know I decided to stay in tonight since I was exhausted from the late night at my parent's house.

I changed into my flannel pajamas with goldfish in top hats and slipped a pair of purple pig slippers onto my feet. I puttered into the kitchen and put some kitty chow down for Ferdie. I opened a can of soup to heat on the stove for dinner. Even though it had been warm the past few days, the evening had grown chilly. I decided to start a fire in the fireplace. I turned the stove to low, then headed into the living room. Dad had brought me a load of wood a few weeks ago. I put a few logs in the grate. It took a few minutes, but once I got a small blaze going, I headed back to the kitchen to eat dinner and enjoy a glass of Cabernet.

The back door opened and Juliet stuck her head in. "Knock knock!"

"Who's there?" I answered.

"Juliet." She knew the drill.

"Juliet, who?" I played along.

"Juliet me in! It's cold outside!" Smiling, she shrugged off her jacket and slung it on the back of one of the kitchen chairs. "What's for dinner? I'm starving!"

"Nothing fancy tonight. Soup from a can. I just finished warming it up on the stove. There's some cheddar cheese in the refrigerator and crackers in the cabinet if you want some to go along with the soup. Open that bottle of wine while you're at it." I pulled out two bowls and filled them with chicken noodle soup. I placed them on the table and grabbed some spoons while Juliet placed the cheese and crackers on a plate for us to share. Pouring a glass of wine for herself and another for me, she sat down.

"So you and Wade, huh?" I tried to sound nonchalant.

"Me and Wade." Juliet nodded her head and ate her soup. I waited for her to say something else, but she suddenly became very interested in the bowl in front of her.

"Oh, heck no! Don't you dare toy with me! I want details! How long have you been dating? Is he romantic? Are you in love?" The questions tumbled out of me.

"Slow down there, PheePhee. You will give yourself a heart attack!" Juliet laughed. "We've dated for almost two months and yeah, it might be love."

"Seriously?! I never thought you'd be interested in a guy like Wade. You're so free spirited and kumbaya. The anti-commitment queen. To be honest, I always pictured you with somebody like Duane living down by the water in a refurbished train car or something," I said only half-jokingly. My sister was always trying out the next New Age trend. Last year she was into crystals and tai chi. This year it was yoga and auras.

"Meh," Juliet shrugged. "Duane and I dated for a week, but he's a little too psychedelic and out there even for me. Wade's a good balance. He's been through a lot in the past couple of years. He says I bring him peace. I don't want to say anything else in case I jinx it. Where's a piece of wood when you need to knock on it." She looked around the kitchen, leaned over and knocked on my wooden cabinets. Ferdie glanced up from his bowl of chow and gave her a disdainful sniff.

"That's great, Juls. Wade is an awesome guy. Don't go breaking his heart. I don't want to lose him as my right hand man at the library. He looks out for me." I stopped and put my hand to my mouth.

"What? What's wrong?" Juliet looked at me with growing concern.

"I might know who killed Huey and Carla," I said slowly.

"What? Who? Phee, what the heck are you talking about?" Juliet demanded.

"I don't know. Chances are I'm wrong. Wade's protective due to his military training. It made me think about someone killing to protect me." I hesitated as I considered my suspicions.

"Are you saying Wade killed them? You're crazy!" Juliet protested.

"No! Not Wade. Someone who is always looking out for me," I said as the idea formed in my head.

"Well, are you going to keep it to yourself or will

you share this brilliant deduction of yours?"

"Believe it or not, it might be Cincinnati." Once I said it out loud, it became concrete for me. Charlie was there in the library when I became angry with Huey Long for grabbing me. Plus, Charlie came to my rescue one time before when Huey made a creepy comment about my legs. He was also outside the library the day Carla was nasty to me. He attended all the town council meetings since he liked to keep up with local politics. It made perfect sense. The icing on the cake was that he was at the fire department's benefit breakfast. It all added up.

"Really? Charlie Cochran? Have you finally cracked, Phee? Charlie is one of the nicest guys in town. Where's your proof?" Juliet looked at me like she wanted to put me in a padded room. I explained to her about Charlie being around when I argued with both of them and how he always looked out for me whenever someone was rude or insulting.

"That's pretty thin. He's a murderer because he's a gentleman and steps in to defend you? With logic like that Clint, Wade, Dad, Rick and a dozen other people should be suspects, too," Juliet argued.

"There's one way to find out," I said.

"How's that?" Juliet asked.

"Investigate!" I announced in triumph hoisting my spoon in the air.

"As long as we don't have to wear those stupid "L" for loser masks," Juliet responded grumpily.

CHAPTER EIGHTEEN

"I can't believe you talked me into this." Juliet pouted in the passenger seat of Velma. "I don't care what you say. Charlie didn't kill anybody. I'm just glad you didn't make me wear that stupid mask. I don't do superheroes."

I was still pouting because Juliet took my mask away from me when I tried to put it on for the drive. "Well, it makes perfect sense. I'm going to go do a little investigation of my own. If I am right, I'll turn it all over to Clint." I got out of Velma and motioned for her to come with me. Reluctantly, she climbed out. She dragged her feet like a two year old and followed behind me as I walked to Charlie's. He lived in a modest ranch-style house a few blocks from me. His lawn was the envy of every gardener in Miller's Cove. His years as the town groundskeeper carried over into his personal life. Everything was immaculate in his yard. Not a blade of grass was taller than what Charlie allowed. I knocked on the door and waited.

"He's not home, so let's go!" Juliet said and turned to head back to the van. I knocked again. From inside, I heard footsteps and a moment later, he opened the door.

"What a surprise! Come in!" Charlie motioned us inside. Juliet gave me a look that could cut diamonds before we followed.

"Come on into the living room. I've got the game playing, but since it's not the Reds, I can miss a few innings for two beautiful girls." He turned the television down and sat down in the recliner. "Have a seat."

Juliet and I sat next to each other on the old, but clean sofa covered by an afghan in hideous shades of orange, yellow and brown. I cleared my throat and wondered how to start.

"We're here collecting for a family over in Hamilton whose house burned down last week," Juliet said. "They needed some men's clothing for the dad and teenage son. Do you have any shoes or jackets you could donate?" I looked at her in surprise. This was brilliant. Juliet missed her calling. She should have been a detective.

"Well, I sure do." Charlie got up from his recliner. "Follow me and I'll see what I have." He ambled down the hallway. Juliet gave me a triumphant look. We followed him down the hall. He opened his closet and looked through his shoes. Glancing over his shoulder, I discovered that Charlie wore a size thirteen shoe and not one pair were sneakers. They were much too large for the shoe print that Deputy Thompson had found. My Super Librarian crime-fighting ego deflated to the size of a peanut.

"Will these do?" Charlie pulled out a pair of construction boots that looked almost new.

"Those would be great," I said feeling guilty knowing there was no family to receive this generous gift.

"I might have a jacket in here, but I don't know. Most of them are in rough shape since I wear them when I am working in my yard." Charlie pushed through his clothes trying to find one to donate.

"These boots will be fine," Juliet said quickly. "Dad said he had some things to donate, so we're going to head over there. I appreciate your generosity."

"You know I would do anything for you girls," Charlie said and patted me on my arm. "I consider the people in this town as my family. Some of them might be a little nuts or not very nice, but it's a great family to have."

This sweet old man couldn't kill anyone. I reached over and hugged him. He looked down at me in surprise. "What was that for?"

"Just a thank you for being such a good friend and all around great guy," I told him. "We'd better get going if we want to make it to my parent's tonight. Thanks again, Charlie. See you tomorrow?"

"Yep. If you gals are heading out, I'll get back to my game. You have a good evening." He headed back to his recliner as Juliet and I left.

Once we were in Velma, Juliet smacked me on the arm. "I told you so. Baby sister sometimes knows best, so nanny nanny boo boo."

"Really? What are you? Two? I'm relieved it isn't him. He really is a nice, old man." I put Velma into gear and headed back home. "Guess I need to rethink my suspects."

"And you need to rethink your superhero costume before you put it on again," Juliet joked. I turned, stuck my tongue out at her and laughed.

CHAPTER NINETEEN

After Juliet left, I put my goldfish pajamas back on and this time chose the skunk slippers. They were my favorite pair. The fire had died down in the fireplace, so I added a few more pieces of wood until it blazed back into life. I perused my shelf and pulled down a Hercule Poirot novel and settled onto the couch to read.

I was immersed in chapter two when Ferdie jumped up on the window sill and yowled. "Knock it off, Ferdie. You're being rude. Can't you see I'm trying to read?" I picked my book back up, but Ferdie persisted. He paced back and forth in front of the window and growled. Who needed a guard dog when they had a twenty-five pound guard cat? I put my book down and went to see what upset him. I peered through the window and spotted a small dog digging in my yard. I hurried out onto the front porch to yell at him before he tore everything up. When I looked out into the yard, I saw a man was bent over and hooking a leash to the little yard destroyer.

"Your dog was digging holes in my yard," I called out. The man stood up and turned. When he did, I realized that it was Clint. "What are you doing out here?"

With a sharp tug on the leash, Clint walked towards me. The little dog wagged his nubby tail. He was a cute little guy despite his dirt-covered paws. "I was out walking Watson. I let him loose at Longfellow Park to run around. He took off like a shot, and I've been chasing him all over the neighborhood. He ended up here. Sorry about the holes in the yard. I'll stop by tomorrow and fill them in and try to patch up the grass."

"Don't worry about it. Watson, huh?" I bent down to pet him on his smooth brown and white head. He gazed at me with his puppy dog eyes.

"From Sherlock Holmes and Watson. My cat's name is Sherlock. This little guy is a Jack Russell Terrier. He's about six months old," Clint said with as much pride as a new dad at the maternity ward.

"He's awfully cute. Do you want to come in the house for a few minutes? I've got some news to tell you anyway." I opened the door. Clint and Watson followed me into the house.

"I see the skunk slippers are back. I like the animal theme you've got going with the feet."

"I've got sexy feet. Tra la la." I did a little two step with my slippers. Watson barked in excitement when he saw the skunk tails wiggle. He leaped forward and attacked the tail. He whipped it off my foot and shook it furiously. Off balance, I fell and hit the ground with my butt and gave a small bounce. "Ouch!"

"Watson, no!" Clint attempted to grab the slipper, but the little terrier growled. Thinking it was a game, he tugged again. Clint picked him up and could finally pry the now mangled slipper from his jaws. He held it out. We burst out laughing.

"I guess we know what Watson's calling in life will

be. Defender of the feet and slayer of stuffed slippers!" I laughed, slipped the skunk back on my foot and stood up. "Come into the kitchen, and I'll get the brave warrior a bowl of water."

I filled a bowl from the sink and set it on the kitchen floor. Ferdie had ventured out from the living room to see what all the fuss was about. When he spotted the little terrier, he stuck his nose in the air and stalked out of the room. Digging holes and fighting vicious skunk slippers was hard work. Watson took three turns around and settled onto the floor with his head on his paws.

"I opened a bottle of wine earlier. Would you like a glass?" I grabbed two glasses and pulled the wine stopper from the bottle.

"I will if you will." Clint walked over and took a glass from me.

"Let's go into the living room. It's chilly tonight. I have a fire going in there already," I said feeling a little bold. It was now or never. I walked into the living room and sat down on the couch. Clint sat down next to me. A few minutes later, there was a clicking of nails on hardwood as Watson followed us. He settled onto the rug in front of the fireplace and closed his eyes to sleep.

"His great escape and subsequent skunk slaying have worn him out," I said.

"I guess so. He's a good little dog. He keeps me company." Clint took a sip of wine. "What's up? You said you needed to tell me something."

"Charlie Cochran isn't the killer," I said. "Juliet and I did some investigating of our own, and we've determined that he cannot be the murderer."

"You what? Of all the crazy stunts why in the world would you investigate Charlie?" Clint gave me an exasperated look. "Listen, Phee. I know you read all these mysteries." He picked up the Hercule Poirot novel I left on the coffee table. He held it up and then shaking his head put it back down. "This is real life though. This isn't some pretend character in a book killing pretend people. Two people have died already. Now is not the time for you to pull out your Junior Girl Detective Kit. Let me handle this."

"I know it's for real," I said indignantly. "I took Juliet with me. It's your fault I went to investigate anyway."

"My fault? How is it my fault?"

"You said that the one thing Huey and Carla had in common is me. Charlie was there both times I argued with them. Plus, he is always jumping in to protect me. He was a logical suspect," I finished. Clint glared at me. He was not impressed with my brilliant detective work. I continued, "Juliet and I went over to his house tonight..."

"You what? Of all the hare-brained ideas! Damn it, Phee!" Clint put the wine glass on the coffee table. He reached over and grabbed me. He gave me an exasperated shake and then with a groan, pulled me to him. His arms crushed me to his chest as he kissed me. Instead of pulling away, I leaned into him. He sensed my need, and his kiss deepened. His hand cupped my breast, and I moaned against him. I had dreamed about this moment for ages. I didn't want to wake up if it wasn't real.

"Phee, do you want me to stop?" Clint asked me. "I can't take much more. I've wanted you for so long."

"Don't stop," I whispered and my hand reached down for the button of his jeans. With a swift movement, he lifted me up into his arms and carried me down the hall to my bedroom. He laid me on the bed and undressed me. My pajamas were slipped off, and I lay naked on the comforter. I reached out my hand to cover myself, but Clint grabbed it and kissed it.

"Don't. I want to see and touch every inch of you." He kissed my shoulder and slowly licked his way across my collar bone until his mouth lit upon my breast. He nibbled gently on it. As I arched my back in pleasure, he stroked his fingers against my thighs. Unable to take anymore, I reached over and tugged at his jeans. He tugged off his shirt and slipped out of his jeans. Clint leaned in and kissed me as I reached for him.

"Are you sure?" Clint gazed down at me with a slight question in his eyes. I nodded, and he parted my thighs with his knees. I gasped. As I rose to meet him, I felt a slow pleasure building. I rode the wave and as he moved a final time, I cried out with pleasure. With a groan, I felt his body shudder. Moments later, he collapsed next to me. He leaned over and kissed me.

"I've wanted to be with you like this for a long time. I wasn't too rough?" Clint asked as he caressed my face.

"I didn't want gentle." I nibbled on his neck and placed tiny kisses along his ear. "I just wanted you."

"It will be better next time," Clint promised.

"Hmmmm...." I snuggled against him.

"Phee..." He pulled me tight against him. At that moment, a jingle sounded from the floor. "I'll ignore that." He kissed me on my neck and earlobe. A moment later, the jingle from his phone rang out again. With a sigh, he leaned down and pulled the phone out of his pants pocket. Looking at the screen, he said, "I'm sorry, Phee, but I've got to answer this. It's Sheriff Dawes." He hit a button and held the phone to his ear.

"Mason." Clint answered. I heard a tinny voice but couldn't make out the words. Clint listened for a moment. "Yes, sir. I'll be right over." He disconnected the call. He stood up and pulled on his jeans. "I'm sorry, Phee, but I've got to go. Normally, Mark would take the call since he's been covering night shift this week, but the Sheriff said he needs me there." He slipped his shirt on over his head. "Can I leave Watson here with you? I can come by and pick him up in the morning."

Feeling awkward and aware of my nakedness, I wrapped the blanket around my body. "Sure. What's happened?"

"I can't get into it right now. I'll come by in the morning before you leave for work." He leaned over and kissed me on the forehead and walked out the door.

CHAPTER TWENTY

After Clint left, I sat there in the dark and thought about what had happened. I was in turmoil. Clint had finally seen me as a woman, but now I wondered if I was just another one of his conquests. I had never seen him with a woman for more than just a few months. Was I just another notch on his gun belt? I was inexperienced with love. Most of what I knew about romance and sex came from the classic movies I watched. I had one serious boyfriend while I was in college. I slept with him after dating him for the entire school year. He dumped me when he returned home for summer break. Ever since then, I'd been skittish about getting physical with a man. I guess I wanted the whole package. I wanted the romance, the starry skies and the gallantry. If I couldn't have it all, then I didn't want to settle for second best.

I pulled on my chenille robe and walked to the kitchen. Watson jumped up and followed me. He gave me an expectant whine. "Sorry, Watson, but I don't have any puppy chow. You could eat a little chicken though, couldn't you?" I grabbed some roast chicken out of the refrigerator and put some on a plate for him. I made myself a cup of lavender tea and then called Juliet. I needed advice.

"Oh my goddess! Do you realize what time it is?" Juliet groaned when she answered the phone. "Somebody better be bleeding or dead or I swear you will be!"

"I slept with Clint," I said.

"Holy cow! Ok. I'll forgive you for waking me up." There was a rustling noise. "No, Wade, no one has died. It's just Phee. Go back to sleep. Hold on, Phee. Let me walk into the other room."

"I'm sorry. I didn't mean to wake you, but I had to talk to someone," I apologized.

"It's okay. I can talk now. What the heck? How did this happen? Rick will kill him!"

"Don't you dare tell Rick!" I admonished her. "Don't tell anyone. Not even Wade. It just kind of happened. One minute he was sitting next to me on the couch, and I was trying to tell him about clearing Charlie from our suspect list. The next minute we were in the bedroom."

"Where is he now?" Juliet asked.

"He got a phone call from Sheriff Dawes and had to leave," I told her. "I don't know, Juliet. What if I am just a one-night stand for him? You know how long I've waited for him to notice me. Now I might be some cheap roll in the hay for him."

"First, no one but Grandma Millie says roll in the hay anymore. Second, I doubt he thinks of you that way. Clint knows you and he knows you don't date much. Oh, who am I kidding? You don't date, period," Juliet reassured me. "We've all noticed how much he's been paying attention to you even though you're oblivious most of the time. He saw the light and realized what an amazing sister I have."

"Thanks, Juls. That makes me feel better, but we

didn't even have time to talk about what happened before the phone rang. Now, I am sitting here in the dark and wondering if I made a mistake." I took a sip of my tea. I heard a noise outside on the front porch, and Watson barked.

"Is that a dog?" Juliet asked.

"It's Clint's. He had to leave in a hurry, and I said I would dog sit until morning. Hold on, Juliet. There's something outside. Whatever it is, it's making Watson go nuts." I laid the receiver down and picked Watson up in my arms. I peered through the entryway window but couldn't see anything. I stepped out on the front porch and looked around the yard, but I still saw nothing. It must have been the wind. I turned to go back inside. I stifled a yelp of surprise. Someone had tacked a white rose to my front door. There was something not quite right. The tips of the rose were red. I realized it was blood dripping off of it and let out a small scream. I ran back into the house and slammed the door shut. Racing down the hall, I picked up the phone.

"What was that, Phee? You screamed!" Juliet shouted into the phone. "What's going on?"

"Wake Wade up and come over right away! Someone just left a bloody rose on my front door. I'm really scared!" I sobbed into the phone.

"What? Hold on. We'll be there in a few minutes. Lock the doors and windows and don't let anybody in. I'll call you from my cell phone when I'm outside your door." Juliet hung up. I checked all the doors and window locks. Once I was sure they were secure, I turned on all the downstairs lights and waited.

CHAPTER TWENTY ONE

I was sitting in the living room wrapped in a blanket trying to get warm next to the fire. My fear had chilled me to my core. Someone hated me enough to leave that on my door. I had Watson in my lap and stroked his velvety ears trying to comfort myself. He pushed his cold little nose against my hand and whimpered.

"Don't worry, little guy. I'll keep you safe," I whispered to him sounding braver than I felt. Ferdie had taken up his post on the windowsill and his tail switched back and forth as he gazed out the window. The telephone on the end table broke the silence. "Hello?"

"It's me, Phee. I'm pulling up right now with Wade. Rick is here, too." Juliet said. "Go ahead and unlock the door." I hurried to the front door and undid the security chain then unlocked the deadbolt. I opened the door and Juliet rushed in and wrapped her arms around me. I sobbed against her shoulder. "It's okay, Phee. It's going to be okay." She stroked my hair.

"Phee, what the hell is going on here?" Rick demanded. He was still in his sweatpants and sports jersey he slept in. His hair was standing on end. His fists opened and closed as he tried to contain his anger. He looked at the rose tacked to the door and spat out a curse. "I'm calling the police."

"I already did," Juliet said. "I called them right before I called you. Sheriff Dawes and Clint are at an active crime scene right now. Janet, the night dispatcher, said she was calling it in to the sheriff. They're sending one of the reserve deputies over to take Phee's statement and collect the evidence. They should be here any minute."

"I will catch whoever played this little joke on you, Phee, and I will beat them senseless," Rick said through gritted teeth. "This is not even funny."

"Calm down, Rick," Wade said. "I don't think threatening to beat someone no matter how much they deserve it is helping the situation. I've got to wonder if this is related to everything else that has been going on in town. First, Huey Long is strangled, and then Carla is poisoned. Now, Phee gets a bloody rose stuck to her door. I've got to tell you. I'm worried. There's a little too much going on and it all seems to center on Ophelia." He nodded in my direction. Juliet tightened her arm around me and shot Wade a warning glance.

"It might be nothing," Juliet reassured me. "Someone is probably starting Halloween pranks a month early. Let's go sit down, Phee, and wait for the deputy."

"I, for one, need a drink," Rick said. He walked over to the antique drinks trolley in the corner of the living room, poured a finger of whiskey and swallowed it in one gulp. He poured another and handed it to me. "Drink it. You're white as a sheet and shaking."

I took the tumbler from him and drank it. The fiery liquid scalded my throat and I gasped. "Thanks," I wheezed out. A knock sounded from the front door. I started to get up, but Rick put up a hand to stop me and went to answer it. He returned moments later with Deputy Sorensen. Dave Sorensen was the high school science teacher, but he was also a reserve deputy. He had been a military policeman in the Marines, so he filled in when necessary.

"Hey there, folks. Phee, I understand this is your house?" He pulled out a notebook to jot down some notes. "Tell me what happened."

"I was sitting in the living room when there was a noise, and Watson started to bark. I went outside to check it out and didn't see anyone. When I turned around to go inside, I found the rose. It had blood or red paint on it. It scared me, so I ran inside and haven't been back outside since," I said. Juliet gave me another hug and a nod of encouragement. "I was already on the phone with Juliet. She, Wade and Rick rushed over here. I didn't see or hear anything else."

"Wait. What are you doing with Clint's dog?" Rick interrupted. Juliet shot him a warning glare. He opened his mouth to say something else and then thought better of it.

"Any enemies? Any recent altercations with anyone? Can you think of any reason someone would play a joke like this on you?" Deputy Sorensen asked.

"I don't think this is a joke," Juliet interjected. "Huey Long and Carla Karsen both argued with Phee before they died and now someone has left this rose on Phee's door as a warning. My sister has no enemies. She is the nicest person I know."

"Is this true, Phee?" Sorensen was jotting something down in his notebook.

"About me arguing with Huey and Carla before they were killed? Yes. About me being the nicest person? I don't know." I gave him a weak smile. "Who would want to scare me like this?"

"I'll take the rose into evidence. It isn't paint on it. It appears to be blood, but what kind I don't know. I'll get it to the lab in the morning, and we'll let you know. In the meantime, can someone stay here with you tonight?" He closed his notebook and looked up at me.

"We'll stay," Wade offered, "if that's okay with you, Phee. Juliet and I can stay, and Rick can head home. He needs to stay with Carrie." Rick gave him a grateful look. Rick had enough on his plate with his wife pregnant with twins. He didn't need to worry about his little sister, too.

"Thanks Wade. I would appreciate it if you would," I said gratefully. "The spare room is already made up. And thank you, Dave, for coming out tonight. It might be nothing, but I have to tell you, it shook me up finding that on my door."

"Not a problem. I'll update the sheriff and someone will be in touch with you in the morning. Keep your doors and windows locked. Try to get some rest." He touched his finger to the brim of his hat, turned and left.

"Well, let's everyone calm down and try to get some sleep. We can deal with everything in the morning," Juliet shot another glance at Rick who was still pacing like a caged tiger. "Rick, head on home to Carrie. She's got to be worried. We'll call you if anything happens."

"You're right. I'd better get back to her. I don't like leaving her alone at night." Rick pushed his fingers through his hair. He looked exhausted. "I still want to know what's going on with you and Clint, but now is not the time or the place. I'm installing an alarm on this house, Phee, and I don't want any argument. Understood?" Rick did a final check of the window locks in the living room. He came over and gave me a hug. "I won't let anything happen to you, PheePhee. I love you. Wade, I'm counting on you to keep my sisters safe."

"I love you, too, Rick. And quit calling me PheePhee," I tried to joke, but it fell flat.

"I will make sure nothing happens to them. I faced worse dangers over in the sandbox. If anyone tries to break in here tonight, they'll be met with a .45 at the door." Wade patted the side pocket of his camos where I now noticed there was a large bulge.

"I'll call you in the morning." Rick turned and left. Wade followed behind him to lock the door.

"Try to get some sleep, Phee. Wade and I will be right in the next room," Juliet reassured me.

"Okay. I doubt I could sleep a wink after this, but I'll take Watson and get under the covers. Thanks for coming to my rescue, Juls." I hugged her and headed towards my bedroom.

"What are sisters for but to ride in and save the day?" Juliet responded.

I headed into my bedroom and checked the window locks one more time before crawling into the bed. I let Watson curl up on the bed next to me. I felt a heavy thump land at the end of the bed. Ferdie decided to share the space with the puppy. I felt him settle on my feet. Surrounded by my furry guardians, I fell asleep moments after closing my eyes.

CHAPTER TWENTY TWO

I awoke to a loud pounding on the front door. I grabbed my robe from the end of the bed and hurried to answer the door. Wade was already there with the gun in his hand. He motioned for me to stay back. Juliet peered around the door of the spare room. Anxiously, we waited as Wade rolled his wheelchair to the door and looked through the front entry window. He relaxed and put the gun down. He reached up, unlatched the chain and unlocked the deadbolt. When he opened the door, Clint charged through like an angry bull bearing down on a toreador. He spotted me standing in the hallway, and in two long strides, he pulled me into his arms.

"Ahem," Wade coughed gently. "Hey there, Clint."

Releasing me, he inspected me up and down. "You aren't hurt? Are you okay? I got here as soon as I could, but I couldn't leave the crime scene."

"I'm fine. Just a little shaken up." I gave him a wan smile to reassure him.

"Wade and I can head home now if Clint will take over Phee duty," Juliet offered. She was subtle. I gave her a grateful look.

"I'm not going anywhere," Clint said. "Thanks for coming by, Wade. I appreciate it. You too, Juliet."

"Not a problem. Phee, I'll work tomorrow for you. You stay home and try to relax." Wade shrugged on his coat and handed Juliet's jacket to her.

"Thanks Wade. I'll take you up on that offer." I hugged Juliet and gave Wade a quick hug of gratitude. "I'll call you if anything happens." I stood at the doorway with Clint until I saw that they had climbed into Wade's car and stowed his chair in the back. Closing the door, I locked it and burst into tears.

Clint picked me up and carried me to the living room. He settled me onto the chaise lounge and wrapped a blanket around me. "I'm going to take Watson out for a minute. I am sure he is about to burst. Then I will make you a cup of tea, and you will tell me everything." I nodded my ascent. He wiped my tears away with his thumb and planted a kiss on the end of my nose. "I'll be right back."

Clint snapped the leash onto Watson's collar and carried him to the kitchen door and out into my fenced in back yard. A few minutes later, I heard him shut and lock the door and the sound of the teapot being filled with water. I wiped my eyes and gave a last little sniffle. So much for my master plan not to turn into a hysterical mess. I probably looked like a naked mole rat - all pink and blotchy with red eyes.

The teapot whistled. A few minutes later, Clint appeared in the doorway with two cups of tea in his hands. He handed me one and settled at the foot of the chaise. Taking a sip, I realized he made it just the way I like with just a touch of honey. After a second sip, I warmed up and told him what happened after he left.

"This is getting too close to you for my comfort," Clint said grimly once I had finished. "I just left the scene of another murder. Someone shot Duane Phillips at close range in his trailer tonight."

"Oh no! Not Duane! He just came and saw me today. I told him you wanted to talk to him. Why in the world would anyone want to kill him? He was the nicest guy." I felt a tear trickle down my cheek. Duane had been my friend. I couldn't believe someone had shot him.

"We believe that someone shot him to keep him quiet. He must have shown someone or given someone the destroying angel mushroom and they used it to kill Carla. We found some in his trailer. Duane was a loose end they couldn't afford. He paid the price with his life." Clint's mouth tightened. "Now I want you to tell me everything you did today. In particular, I want to know about you and Juliet's investigation into Cincinnati."

I told him all about my visit with Charlie at his house. I explained how Charlie had been present when I had argued with both Huey and Carla, so it made sense that he killed them to protect me. "But his feet are too big," I finished.

"What? What are you talking about?"

"The footprints outside Mr. Long's house were not very big. Juliet told Charlie that we were collecting clothes and shoes for a family in need. He wears a size thirteen shoe. From what we could tell, he doesn't own any tennis shoes. It can't be him."

"Did you ever think someone besides the murderer left those footprints outside Huey's house? And maybe, Charlie might still be a suspect. Of all the ridiculous things you and Juliet have done over the years, I think this one takes the cake!" Clint gave me an exasperated look.

"No," I said in a small voice. "But he's such a nice man. I hope it isn't him."

"Well, luckily for you and Juliet, it isn't. Charlie had an alibi for tonight's murder. It turns out that Si Kaminski's cable went out tonight. He walked next door to Charlie's house to finish watching the baseball game. He stayed until well after midnight since the game went into extra innings. Duane was killed sometime between 8 p.m. and 10 p.m. He wouldn't have had time to kill Duane and drive all the way back across town to his house before Si walked over at 8:15. Charlie was one of the first people we talked to tonight since he let Duane park his camper in the woods behind his house. He's not a suspect."

"Juliet and I left Charlie's house around 7:45 if that helps any," I offered. I tried to imagine how anyone could kill peace-loving Duane and felt an overwhelming sadness when I realized I wouldn't see him around town anymore.

"Well, that clears Charlie, then. Duane's place is at least a ten minute walk through the woods from Charlie's in broad daylight. In the dark, it would take at least twenty minutes. Plus, Charlie's knocking on seventy years old. Duane might be a stoner, but he was fit from all of his hiking and rock-climbing."

"I'm glad it's not Charlie," I said. "I like him, and he looks out for me."

"I am, too. But now we have a bigger problem,"

Clint said.

"What?" I asked.

"Whoever killed Huey and Carla to protect you changed the game by killing Duane. And even more concerning is I believe that something else has changed. The bloody rose was a warning. I don't think whoever is doing these killings is looking out for you anymore, Phee. I think you've become their next target."

CHAPTER TWENTY THREE

I looked at Clint with horror. "Do you believe that? I mean, why would anyone want to come after me?"

"To be honest, I don't know. Duane's murder and now this blood-covered rose left for you tells me that everything is tied to you," Clint said grimly. He pulled me closer to him. "I will do my damnedest to make sure nothing happens to you."

"I just can't imagine anyone I know doing these horrible things to Huey, Carla and now Duane. It has to be someone new to Miller's Cove, or someone just passing through town. Have they figured anything out with Huey or Carla's murders?"

"We should have the last of the reports back from Carla's autopsy tomorrow. The preliminary results showed the cause of death was the poisonous mushroom. This final report was the only thing we were still waiting on. It will tell us how much of the deadly mushroom killed her and verify it was during the benefit breakfast. The problem is that so many people were there," Clint said.

"It had to be someone who was preparing the food, wouldn't it? I mean, it's not like she wouldn't have noticed somebody drop the mushrooms onto her plate," I reasoned. "That should narrow it down."

"Well, you would think so but there were several people helping out on the serving line. And with that big of crowd, they could wait for Carla to turn her head to talk to someone. They could drop it into her food and she'd be none the wiser. It's like finding a needle in a haystack except this needle is deadly," Clint said. "I just know that I am tired and frustrated with our lack of leads."

I rested my head against his chest. Before tonight, I had always felt safe in Miller's Cove. Juliet and I thought nothing about walking around in Longfellow Park at midnight. Most residents still left their doors unlocked at night. Our little town was changing and not in a good way. "Can I ask you something?"

"Sure," Clint said.

"What's happening with you and me? I mean, not that I expect anything or..." I trailed off unsure I wanted to hear his answer.

"Phee, can't you tell how I feel about you? I've just been waiting for you to open your eyes and stop seeing me as Rick's buddy who gave you rides on his dirt bike. I got tired of waiting for you to get a clue." He leaned in and kissed me gently.

"I've been waiting for you to stop seeing me as the little girl in pigtails who begged you for that ride on the bike." I shook my head in disbelief.

"I know that you aren't that same little girl. I believe I covered that earlier this evening," Clint said huskily as he kissed me again. "And I plan on staying right here with you tonight to keep you safe." He stood up and I followed him to the bedroom.

I woke up the next morning to the smell of fresh coffee. I opened my eyes and found Clint wearing my blue chenille robe and holding two cups of coffee. I sat up and he handed one of the cups.

"You look good in blue," I smiled at him. "I hope you didn't wear my skunk slippers."

"I tried, but they didn't fit. I've got to get going, Phee. I'm supposed to meet with Doc Thompson over at the hospital to get the initial autopsy results on Duane and pick up a copy of Carla's reports." Clint took off the robe and pulled on his discarded clothes. "I've got to drop Watson off at my house first and change clothes. I'm already running late."

"I'm sorry. I didn't mean to make you stay here with me."

"I'm not sorry." He leaned over and gave me a quick, hard kiss. He took a quick sip of coffee before setting the cup on my nightstand. "I'm just sorry that I can't stay longer. I want you to lock the door behind me and stay put today. If you have to go somewhere, make Rick or Juliet take you."

"Okay. I think I will stick close to home today. Can you call me later and let me know what Doc said?"

"I will if I can. Just promise me you'll leave the investigating to me." He gave me another quick kiss and left the bedroom. He whistled for Watson, and I heard the front door open. "Lock the door!" A moment later the door shut, and he was gone. Sighing, I got up and pulled on the discarded robe. Clint's scent clung to the fabric and I inhaled trying to recapture last night. I locked the front door and then headed to the kitchen with my cup. I poured a fresh cup of coffee from the still warm percolator and added cream and sugar. Clint had left the morning paper on the table. I glanced down, and the headlines printed in large, bold letters, "Local Naturalist Shot Dead in Home!" I sat down to read the article. "Local naturalist and food activist, Duane Phillips, was gunned down outside his trailer last night. Sheriff Dawes said that Phillips was shot at close range with what appears to be a .45 caliber handgun. Phillips was active in the community and was vocal in his opposition to construction near the lake and forest. He chained himself to a tree near a proposed subdivision claiming that the area was the home of the endangered New England Silt Snail. 'We are investigating Mr. Phillips movements over the past few weeks to decide if his recent activist campaigns might have contributed to his death,' said Sheriff Dawes. 'We are also interested in speaking with anyone who had contact with the victim yesterday.' Anyone with information is asked to contact the sheriff's department at once." A photograph of Duane chained to a large oak tree accompanied the article.

I sighed and thought about how passionate Duane was about nature and foraging for food. His presentation at the library was well-attended. He brought several species of wild plants in and showed them during his talk.

Slowly, it dawned on me. Duane had several species of mushrooms with him that day. They had been on display on a large table. It would have been easy for someone to walk up and swipe one off the table after the demonstration. We all milled around and chatted over the coffee and cookies the Friends of the Library ladies brought in for the talk. No one would have noticed one go missing.

I sipped my coffee and tried to remember who had stayed after Duane's talk. But if the murderer had taken the mushroom with no one noticing why would they need to kill Duane? Maybe the murderer asked one too many questions and aroused Duane's suspicions.

"Ferdie, I might be trapped in the house, but I can still investigate." I scratched him between his ears, and he purred with pleasure. All was forgiven for allowing the evil little dog into the house his mews of pleasure said. I grabbed a notebook and pen from the desk in my small office, then sat back down at the table. I took another sip of coffee to jump start my memory. "Now, I just need to remember who came that day." I scribbled down the names of potential suspects.

CHAPTER TWENTY FOUR

Fifteen minutes later, I had ten names on my list. My mom had brought Shari Davis with her. I felt safe eliminating them from my suspects. I also marked off two middle-school kids whose moms had dropped them off at the library to get them out of their hair for an hour. That left Charlie, Reverend Taylor and his wife, Patricia, Mike Johnson who owned the local pickle factory, Chris Karsen and Mrs. Grimes. Since Mrs. Grimes was approaching eighty and used a walker, I scratched her off the list, too. My list of possible suspects had narrowed. Satisfied, I puttered around and cleaned my house. By eleven o'clock, I was going stir-crazy.

I had promised Clint I wouldn't go anywhere without Rick or Juliet. Rick worked in the city as an architect, so I couldn't ask him to come babysit me. Juliet was a freelance photographer, yoga instructor, tarot card reader and everything else that didn't need a 9-to-5 schedule. I called her to come rescue me.

"Can you pick me up?" I asked her when she finally answered her phone.

"What time is it?" Juliet asked me. Her voice was groggy with sleep.

"It is almost eleven o'clock in the morning, sleepy head. I came up with a list of possible suspects in the murder of Carla Karsen. Clint has me under house arrest unless you or Rick can babysit. Come break me out, and I'll buy you breakfast." Juliet had the metabolism of a shrew so I the promise of food would get her up and out of bed.

"House arrest, huh? He's progressed to handcuffs with you already?"

"You are hilarious. You should give up yoga and go on tour with a troupe of clowns. Will you come get me? We can go by Nellie Jo's. She should have all things pumpkin since it is fall. I know how much you love her pumpkin spice coffee. I'll even buy you a muffin to eat," I cajoled.

"Fine. Give me a half an hour to get dressed. Do I need to bring handcuff keys?" Laughing, she hung up. I showered and dressed quickly. I pulled my hair up into a messy ponytail and was pulling on my favorite pair of vintage turquoise cowboy boots when a honk sounded from a car horn. I finished slipping the boots on, grabbed my favorite navy blue pea coat and headed to the door. Juliet waited for me in Ole Blue. I hopped in and we drove the short distance to Nellie Jo's Cup o' Joe.

Nellie Jo's was the hot spot in Miller's Cove. Everyone went there to get the latest gossip. It also served muffins the size of grapefruits. She called them moose muffins. Nellie and her husband, Mike, had moved to Miller's Cove from down south over twenty years ago to take over the failing pickle factory. Nellie hated working in the office of the factory, so Mike bought her the coffee shop to make her happy.

Juliet and I walked in and went to the counter area to give our order. It was decorated in twentieth century kitsch. Collectible glasses from the eighties lined shelves along the back wall. Bobble heads decorated the counters and bobbed in unison whenever someone opened the door and let in even a hint of a breeze. A large wooden barrel filled with pickles from her husband's pickle factory sat in front of the counter. I kept waiting for Nellie to introduce a pickle-flavored muffin, but so far she had resisted. I loved coming here.

"Hey, Nellie!" I called out to her. Nellie was clearing coffee cups from a vacated table. Juliet and I took a seat at the counter.

"Hey there, Phee! I'll be with you in a minute. Let me just run these cups to the back." She bumped the swinging doors to the kitchen open and disappeared. A moment later she reappeared and wiping her hands on a bar towel said, "What can I get for you this morning?"

"I think I'll take one of those yummy pumpkin scones and a pumpkin spice coffee with cream. Juliet, what do you want?"

"I'll take a wild blueberry moose muffin and a pumpkin spice coffee, too. No cream for me though." Juliet stifled a yawn.

"You girls have a late night?" Nellie peered at us through her granny glasses. Her nose for gossip must be on high alert.

"Nothing much. Just worried about all these murders going on," I answered casually setting the bait and waiting for her to take it.

"Oh my gosh! I know! Can you believe it? Huey Long strangled in his own home!" Her voice lowered to a confidential whisper. "They discovered him naked."

"Really?" I tried to appear surprised. "I didn't know him all that well. I saw him when he came into the library. He was a bit of a creep to me. He hit on me all the time."

"Well," Nellie continued, "he used to be famous and had all sorts of women sniffing around him. It was probably because of all his money. He wasn't much in the looks department. But once he got out of the business, his luck with the ladies dried up." She poured our coffee.

"If he was famous, how come I never heard of him?" Juliet asked skeptically. "Was he on television or something?"

"Nope. Better. He was a midget wrestler over in Burlington. I can't believe you don't recognize him. Huey the Horrible?" Juliet and I both shook our heads. "Why, me and Mike used to go watch them midget wrestlers every weekend. It was better than that fake stuff on TV. I bet you anything one of his old rivals came and put the killer anaconda choke hold on him and tried to cover it up by strangling him with a belt. Poor little feller."

"Well, he wasn't that old, so how come he stopped wrestling?" I asked.

"He hurt his back real bad. Ivan the Terrible Two-Footer did a back breaker on him, and Huey got all tore up. Had to stop wrestling. He had blown most of the money he had made on cheap women and beer. He moved here to Miller's Cove and lived off what money he got from disability. It's a shame. He was really something fierce in the ring." Nellie smiled at the memory.

"But if a rival killed Huey, then why would they kill Carla, too?" I fished for more gossip.

"That girl was faster than a cheetah on the African savannah. If it had pants, she tried to catch it!" Nellie harrumphed in disapproval.

"Really? Do tell." Juliet leaned forward encouragingly.

"I bet you anything her husband bumped her off for cheating on him. Either that or an angry wife. Rumor is he was prowling around with that Grant Davis not two days after he moved back into town. I guarantee his mama was fit to be tied and put a stop to that real quick." Nellie said.

"Grant?" I was shocked. There had been no love lost between Carla and Grant, but he'd been gone for several years. How well did I know him?

"Yep. Of course, she was also stepping out with Sheriff Dawes. You let Sheila ever find out that Jaime cheated on her, and I guarantee you that Jaime will wake up to find a shotgun aimed at his business!" Nellie declared as she pretended to aim a shotgun and shoot downward.

"Sheila won't hear it from me," I reassured her. "How did Mike like our nature class we had the other day at the library? I was glad to see him take a break from the factory."

"He said he really enjoyed it. He went to learn a

little before going on our fall camping trip with our grandson, Joey. Mike isn't an outdoorsy kind of fella. He prefers sitting in front of the TV with a can of beer watching the game to enjoying the great outdoors. When I asked him what he'd learned, he said he couldn't remember much except to say that now he is scared to eat any kind of mushroom since Duane showed them so many poisonous ones. Real sad what happened to that boy, too. I swear the crime from the big cities is coming here. Can't even be safe in your home at night anymore without someone trying to rob you. Why...I told Mike that we're gonna need to lock all our doors and windows just to feel safe in our own homes. Crying shame if you ask me." Nellie shook her head in dismay.

I took a last bite of my scone and sipped my coffee. "How is your grandson, Nellie?"

"He's doing real good. Made straight A's this marking period. Smart as a whip. He will be running this town one day, mark my words." Her pride in her grandson was evident. "He loves going to the library. Every week he says to me, 'Mamaw, take me to see Miss Phee at the library.' I think he has read every book in there."

"Just about! Well, you bring him by to visit me this week. I have a new series he might like to read. We'd better get going." I stood up to leave. Juliet took a last swallow of her coffee and slipped off her stool to follow.

"You girls stay out of trouble and I'll see you later," Nellie said as we started out the door.

"See you later, Nellie. Thanks for the coffee," I said over my shoulder as we left.

Juliet and I walked to her car and got in. Juliet turned and looked at me and said, "Midget wrestling? Really?" She burst out laughing and I joined her. Minutes later we were still laughing with tears streaming down our faces as we headed towards home.

CHAPTER TWENTY FIVE

Juliet steered Ole Blue down Main Street. The lone stoplight in town turned red, and she slowed to a stop. Our laughter subsided to an occasional snort and giggle. I wiped the tears from my eyes and glanced out the passenger window. I spotted Clint walking into Maybe Baby, the new boutique baby store.

"Pull in to that parking spot up ahead," I demanded.

"What's up?" Juliet pulled the car into the parking spot a few buildings down from the baby boutique.

"Clint walked into Maybe Baby Boutique. Doesn't seem like his kind of store. I want to know what's up," I said and peered through the windshield of the convertible trying to glimpse Clint inside the store.

"We could get out of the car and go in there like normal people," Juliet suggested.

"No way!" I protested. "I don't want Clint to think I am following him or anything."

"Because sitting in a car trying to spy on him isn't following him? And you say I'm the flake?" The sarcasm wasn't wasted on me. I shot her a look.

"I'm not spying on him. I want to check on what he's investigating," I said innocently. "I mean, how am I going to figure out who's committed the murder if I don't keep up with the investigation?"

Juliet snorted in disbelief. "Well, your chief

investigator walked out the door of the store and is heading back towards his car." I sank down in my seat so he wouldn't spot me. I tried to tug Juliet down next to me, but she gave me a look that said I had lost my mind somewhere between Crazy Street and Insane Avenue.

"Is he gone?" I asked. Sliding back up, I peered down the street and watched Clint's patrol car pull out. "Let's go check out the store. We can figure out what he was up to."

"Well, I need to get something for the twins," Juliet said. We hopped out of the car and headed into the store.

When I opened the door to the boutique, the chime rang out *Brahms's Lullaby*. A slight hint of talcum powder and lavender scented the air. The walls were sky blue with fluffy clouds. Paintings of cherubic-faced infants holding balloons drifted among the clouds. A beautiful rocking chair with a hand-carved back in the shape of a cow jumping over the moon sat in the corner of the store. I gravitated towards it. I touched the smooth, light wood and traced the design with my fingertips.

"This is gorgeous!" I exclaimed. "It's perfect for the twins' nursery."

"It's one of a kind," a voice spoke from behind me. Turning, I faced an attractive woman with brunette hair cut into a modern bob and dark brown eyes. I recognized her. Valerie Clark. She was Clint's ex-girlfriend from school.

"Ophelia Jefferson?" Valerie's eyes widened. "Oh

my goodness! You haven't changed since high school."

Inwardly, I rolled my eyes since my teens were the most humiliating and awkward period of my life. Outwardly, I pasted on a fake smile and said with my voice dripping honey, "Valerie Clark. I barely recognized you! How are you?"

"It's Valerie Hill now. I'm doing well."

"Oh? You're married?" I tried to suppress the hope in my voice. Clint and Valerie were the "it couple" back in the day.

"Divorced. I just moved back from New York and opened this boutique to bring a little of the big city to this town." Valerie gave a smug smile.

"Well, it's great! I'm Phee's sister, Juliet. You probably don't remember me." Juliet smiled and held out her hand to Valerie. "Phee and I love this rocking chair. You remember our brother, Rick? He and his wife are expecting twins and the rocker is perfect for the nursery."

"How exciting! Rick's a great guy. I spent a lot of time with Clint and him. Oh, the trouble the three of us got up to when we were kids!" She gave a throaty laugh. "Make sure you tell Rick that Val said hello and congratulations. If you'd like to buy the rocker, I can have it delivered to their home," Valerie offered. "So, Phee, still single?"

"Yep. I'm still single." I gave a forced laugh.

"Well, sometimes you have to wait for the right guy to come along. Or the right guy to come back," Valerie advised. My heart sank. She must be talking about

Clint. I felt like a second hand pair of loafers next to a pair of Manolo Blahnik's. I couldn't compete against Valerie for Clint's affection. She had beauty and sophistication. I was a small town girl who wore funny animal slippers and watched old movies by herself on a Friday night.

"Phee, let's buy the rocker and have it shipped to Mom and Dad's for the baby shower next week," Juliet suggested completely clueless to my inner turmoil.

"Can you take care of it and I'll meet you in the car?" I handed her my credit card.

"Sure." She took my card and headed to the register. I headed out the door with tears stinging my eyes.

Ten minutes later, Juliet opened the car door and climbed into Ole Blue. She looked at my tear-stained face. "What in the world is wrong with you? One minute you're excited about the rocker and the next thing I know, I find you sitting in the car blubbering."

"Don't you remember? Valerie is Clint's high school sweetheart. They were homecoming king and queen. And she's single!" I wailed.

"Oh my goddess! So what? That was ages ago," Juliet gave me an exasperated look. She started Ole Blue and pulled away from the curb. "You're tired and not thinking straight. Clint cares about you. I don't think he is the type to hop out of your bed and straight into Valerie's. Give the guy a little credit. He stopped in to say hello to an old friend. Whoopity doo!"

"But she's pretty and didn't you hear what she said? Wait for the right guy to come back?" I wailed again.

"And you are gorgeous. I don't know why you're always down on yourself. Why don't you ask Clint about today? You might be surprised by the answer."

"But what if I don't like what he says? What if he says he's had a change of heart?" I sniffled.

"And what if he says what I will say? That you have flipped your lid! Talk to him." Juliet pulled Ole Blue up to my house. We got out, and I trudged up the steps. "Come on, PheePhee. It'll be fine. Let's turn on an old movie, mix up a pitcher of Cosmopolitans and relax. I'll let you pick."

"It's one o'clock in the afternoon. I think it's just a tad early for cocktails."

"Not after the week we've had. We'll have a girl's afternoon. I'll call Wade and ask him to pick us up dinner when he gets off work. We can camp out here tonight," Juliet suggested. "We'll eat Chinese food, drink silly girly drinks and make Wade wait on us all night. It'll be fun."

"Alright," I said begrudgingly. I tossed my keys and bag on the small bench by the front door. Kicking off my shoes, I walked into the kitchen to make the pitcher of Cosmos.

"You get to pick between Katherine Hepburn and Audrey Hepburn." Juliet walked into the kitchen holding two movies.

"I feel like kicking butt, so Katherine." I added the vodka to the pitcher, thought about it and poured in a smidgen more. Pouring some into a martini glass, I sipped it. "Perfect!" I placed the pitcher and two martini glasses on an old silver-plated tray and carried them to the living room. Juliet started the movie and the opening credits for *Adam's Rib* scrolled across the screen. I sipped my drink and stewed. "Valerie has a lot of nerve coming back to town and sniffing around Clint."

"Ok," Juliet said. "She might be, but it doesn't mean he's interested. I saw the way he looks at you. He is a man on the verge." I swallowed the remains of my glass, grabbed the pitcher and poured myself another. Juliet raised her eyebrows at me.

"Well, I just offered myself up to him like a sacrificial lamb. He will toss me aside like an old newspaper. I was a fool for thinking he'd be interested in someone like me. I'm going to just forget about Clint Mason and move on," I declared and raised my glass in a toast. "To moving on!"

"Let's put that thought on hold and watch the movie. You are turning into such a drama queen." Juliet kicked off her shoes and stretched out on the chaise lounge. I propped my feet onto the coffee table and stared sulkily at the television as Katherine Hepburn and Spencer Tracy sparred on the screen.

A little over an hour later, the movie was over, and Juliet was snoring like a freight train. I picked up the empty pitcher and carried it to the kitchen. A knock sounded on the door and I opened it to find Clint.

"Howdy, cowboy!" I slurred a little. I shouldn't have drank so much of the pitcher. I giggled.

"Phee, you didn't check before you opened the door," Clint admonished. He took the pitcher out of my hand and steered me towards the kitchen. "I assume Juliet stopped by today."

"We had a girl's afternoon!" I hiccupped and giggled again. Clint sniffed the pitcher and shaking his head set it on the counter. I leaned against him and wrapped my arm around his neck. "But we could let boys into our clubhouse if they promise to behave. No Valerie's allowed in the club though." I slapped my hand over my mouth.

Clint glanced at me sharply. "Valerie? What about her?"

"I saw you go into her store. But I wasn't sp...spy...following you." I hiccupped. "Juliet and I went to Nellie Jo's for a late breakfast and saw you go visit her. I mean if you want to date other people, then I am not the girl for you. Just break it to me. I'm a freakin' Super Librarian. I can handle anything. I gotta mask and stuff." I hiccupped again.

"So you saw me go into Maybe Baby and assumed I went there to see another woman? What kind of man do you think I am, Phee?" Clint demanded with a hint of anger. "For your information, I didn't go to see Valerie. I went there to order a double bassinet for the twins. Rick asked me to do it since he didn't have a chance to go by there. Are you jealous of a girl I dated in high school? That was how many years ago?"

"No...maybe....ok, yes," I admitted. "I'm sorry, but I wasn't following you. We were driving down the street and watched you go into the store. And well...Valerie is all sophisticated and pretty and you used to be in love with her."

"Now I'm not. I'm also not a sixteen-year-old boy high on hormones." He gave an exasperated sigh. "Phee, I don't play games. I'd like it if you didn't either. And besides, my girl," Clint pulled me close to him, "is sexy and smart and funny. She wears smoking hot fuzzy animal slippers, too. Who could compete with all this?" He trailed kisses along my ears and neck.

"I'm your girl?" I asked.

"Most definitely." He leaned in and captured my mouth with his.

CHAPTER TWENTY SIX

Clint's kiss left me a little breathless. "I've got to go back to work. I just came by to check on you. Next time, you need to check first before you answer the door. Okay?"

"I will. Before you go, I have something to show you. I came up with suspects for you." I walked over to the table and handed him the list of people I had written down that morning. "These are all the people that came to Duane's lecture. He had all sorts of mushrooms there, poisonous and edible. It would have been easy for someone to come by, pick one up and take it with them."

"Well, this saves me a step. I planned to go to the library this afternoon and grab the sign in sheet from Wade. The bad thing is that Duane gave talks all the time. There is no guarantee they learned about this lethal mushroom at one of his talks or if they were like your uncle and just ran into him in the woods and struck up a conversation."

"Possibly, but you'll check out the names on the list won't you? I already marked my mom and Shari off the list. I can vouch for them. Juliet and I did a little investigating of our own. Mike Johnson might be in the clear. He went to the lecture to learn a bit about wild plants to try to bond with his grandson. Joey's been trying to earn his scout badges. It's all he talks about when he comes in the library with Nellie."

"What investigating did you and Juliet do?" Clint asked.

"We just talked to Nellie while we had coffee. She knows everything about everyone in town. The C.I.A. could take lessons from her. I asked her how Mike had liked Duane's presentation. Nellie told me he liked it but mostly went to learn a little before the camping trip. Did you realize that Huey Long was a famous midget wrestler?" I thought that snippet of gossip might surprise him.

"Yep, sure did." He tapped his badge. "That's why I make the big bucks as a deputy sheriff. I'm more than just a pretty face. I even investigate now and then, little darlin'." He chuckled and pretended to tip his hat.

"It was news to me," I pouted. "I guess I need to go to Nellie Jo's more often to keep up with what's going on in town. Who knew we had a star in our midst? Okay, Mr. I Know Everything, were you aware Carla cheated on Chris? Nellie told us that Carla was messing with Sheriff Dawes. Maybe Sheila killed Carla as payback for messing with her man."

"That little piece of gossip isn't all true. Sheila and Jaime were going through a rough patch awhile back. Carla wanted Jaime on her side with the town council. She tried to seduce him, but Jaime put the brakes on her little plan. I was in the office when he told her that he wasn't interested. I worried the windows might shatter when she slammed out of his office," Clint said.

"That makes me feel better. Sheila and my mom are friends, and I've known Jaime and her forever. Nellie also let it slip that Grant and Carla were messing around," I said. "I will figure out a way to ask Grant. We've always been close, but I guess not as close as we used to be. He used to hate Carla."

"Oh, hell no! Absolutely not! You will not ask Grant anything." Clint's voice was emphatic and his arm tightened slightly around me.

"Jealous?" I teased and kissed him.

"This time, no. I'm worried about keeping you safe which I am realizing might be a full-time job. I might be wrong, but Grant has an interest in you which ties him to Huey and Carla. He was friends with Duane and admits he spent hours out in the woods as kids with him. Phee, he's your friend but let me do more checking into what he's been up to the past few years since he left town." Clint's face was stern, and I realized how serious he was.

"Grant wouldn't hurt a fly. He and I practically lived in each other's homes growing up. There is no way he could kill anybody!" I protested.

"Just give me a day or two to check him out. Listen. I've got to get going. I'll stop by again this evening when I get off work." He gave me one last kiss and headed towards the door. "And lay off the Cosmos!" The door shut, and I locked it behind him.

"Was that Clint?" Juliet said. Her voice was groggy from sleep.

"Yes. He stopped by to check up on me."

"Guess he isn't quite as interested in Valerie as you suspected," Juliet said wryly. She trudged into the kitchen. "I need coffee. Wade should be here soon with

138

dinner and to help with bodyguard duty." She scooped coffee into the percolator, added water and plugged it in.

"Jaime wasn't cheating on Sheila. Clint cleared up that rumor. He said that he wanted to do a little checking up on Grant." I pulled cream and sugar out for the coffee.

"Why? Does he think Grant has something to do with the murders?" She poured coffee into our mugs.

"He said he just wants to check him out since he knows me and that ties him to Carla and Huey. Clint's stretching the truth because he doesn't want to admit he is jealous." I took a sip of coffee and grimaced. Juliet made coffee so strong it ate the enamel off my teeth. I added a second scoop of sugar and poured in more cream.

"He might be right," Juliet said. "Think about it. He moves back to town about two months ago. He had a fling with Carla and she dumped him. There's his motive right there."

"To kill Carla, but why would he kill Huey?" I shook my head. Grant couldn't be the killer.

"I'm not sure, but you should let Clint do the investigating. Real life isn't like your books, Phee," Juliet admonished me.

"No, you're right. Books are better!"

CHAPTER TWENTY SEVEN

Juliet and I settled back onto the couch. She dozed lightly while watching a talk show about cheating spouses and their love child. I picked up the Agatha Christie novel from the evening before and tried to read but my mind kept straying towards what Clint had said about Grant. Could Grant kill someone who had threatened me? He was really protective of me in high school. If anyone bullied me, he would always come charging to my rescue. It boggled my mind he slept with Carla. I hoped Nellie had that tidbit of gossip wrong, too. I just wasn't sure what to think anymore. My eyes started to drift shut. I was so tired. I moved over to the chaise lounge and settled in for a nap.

I awoke to the sound of Juliet laughing in the kitchen. I heard Wade's deep voice rumbling and her giggly response. It was good to see Wade happy. I just hoped Juliet wouldn't break his heart. She wasn't known for sticking with a relationship for very long. Wade was a good guy. I heard another male voice talking softly in the kitchen. I rose and ran my fingers through my strawberry curls. I wandered into the kitchen to find Juliet, Wade and Grant opening containers of Chinese food.

"Hey, Phee!" Wade smiled at me. "I got you Moo Shoo Pork. It's what I usually order, and since Juliet said you would eat anything, I figured it was a safe bet. I ran into Grant when I was picking up dinner at the Dragon Palace." Wade scooped out some rice and dumped it on a plate. "I told him what happened last night. He offered to come hang out with us and perform guard duty, too."

"I wish I would have known about all this, Phee. I would have camped out here last night and made sure nothing else happened. I'm just glad you're okay. I'm still reeling from the news that Duane was killed. He was the coolest guy and a good friend. It's crazy that someone would kill him. I moved back home to what was a safe little town, and now people are being killed left and right. Now you're getting weird threats." Grant shook his head. "All these murders and threats are just unbelievable. If anything else happens, you'd better call me."

"I will!" I said with a false brightness. "Juliet, can you come see me in the bedroom for a minute. I need to ask you a question about...um...about this paint color I am considering." I gestured for her to follow me. Once we were out of earshot, I grabbed her arm and hissed, "Oh my gosh! What if Clint's right being suspicious of Grant? I mean, he has been gone for years and when he comes back into town, people do start keeling over."

"Well, it would've been more suspicious if I hadn't let him in. We've known him for years. He was your best friend. Do you really think he could hurt somebody?" Juliet's whisper increased in volume. I shushed her.

"No, but I didn't think he would sleep with Carla either."

"What's going on?" Wade walked into the bedroom.

"Clint is suspicious of him. Grant might have had

something to do with the murders," I whispered. "Now I am paranoid to be around Grant and you invited him to dinner!"

"I'll be here, and I still have a little friend right here." Wade turned and showed me where he had a gun tucked into the waistband of his pants. He pulled the edge of his shirt back over and it was once again hidden from sight. "Let's get back in there before he suspects something." We walked back to the kitchen trying not to appear worried we may be eating dinner with a crazed murderer.

"I had a wild idea to paint my room bright peach, but Juliet talked me out of it," I lied. I grabbed the plate he handed to me and put some Moo Shoo Pork on it. I sat down beside him and opened a pair of paper-wrapped chopsticks.

"Crisis averted!" Juliet chimed in and speared a piece of broccoli with her fork. "What's up with you, Grant?"

"I've been getting settled into the new job and taking on a bunch of new cases. I've tried to get Mom out of the house some more. She wants you to come visit her, Phee. She says she misses us hanging around the house," Grant said.

"I'll have to go by and visit her. I always liked hanging out with your mom. She's a hoot. Remember when she and your dad took us to shoot skeet? I about shot my foot off and ended up accidentally shooting the windows out of the lighthouse. Your mom said I should stick with water pistols." I laughed at the memory. Grant's mom always made time for me when I went there after school with Grant. She baked cookies and sat down and chatted with us. My mom's great, but she and Dad's teaching schedule didn't leave a lot of down time to spend time with us kids except on the weekends.

"She's always been a crack shot. I'm not too bad myself," Grant said with a touch of pride. "I was on the skeet shooting team at university."

"Really? How cool! I never pegged you and your mom as gun people," Juliet said. She gave me a look and continued, "So, Grant, have you been seeing anybody since you've been back?" I kicked her under the table and was glad to see her wince a little when my foot found its target.

"I've gone on a date or two," he said. "Nobody that I would say is a keeper. I'm keeping my options open. I don't think I'm ready for the white picket fence, two kids and a dog named Skipper, but someday I will be. Mom's driving me crazy asking me when I'm going to settle down and give her grandkids. It's times like this I wish I had a brother or sister to distract her."

"Thank goodness we have Rick to distract Mom," Juliet joked. Juliet impressed me with how she managed to ask Grant about his love life. I sat there wanting to ask him if it was Carla or not. I didn't have to though. Juliet gave him a bold smile and asked, "Is this woman you've been dating anyone we would know?" My eyes widened.

Grant pushed a few grains of rice around his plate as he took his time answering. "To be honest, she was married. I'll keep that little indiscretion's name to myself if that's okay, Juliet. She wasn't someone I cared for anyway." I shifted uncomfortably in my seat as I felt his gaze land on me.

"Ladies, enough with the third degree of Grant," Wade said. "Did you catch the game last night? I can't believe that fly ball to left field."

"No. Sorry, I missed out. I heard it was a great game. I was stuck in the office until after midnight going through a case preparing for trial." Juliet and I looked at each other. She was thinking what I was thinking.

"That's too bad you missed the game. I tried calling you last night since I was too tired to have dinner with you. I couldn't reach you," I said with a casual "we're just chatting" tone. I wanted to grab a spotlight and interrogate him like they did in the movies. Tie him to a chair and threaten him with bamboo under the fingernails. I could feel the hairs on the back of my neck tingling as my Super Librarian senses activated.

"Sorry. My cell phone died and I didn't have my charger with me. There was no one but me in the office. Once the secretary left for the day, the phones went straight to voice mail," Grant explained.

I swallowed hard. Grant had no alibi for the murder of Duane. He probably slept with Carla. He represented Huey Long. There was no doubt about it. I shared Chinese food and chopsticks with a murderer.

CHAPTER TWENTY EIGHT

I lost my appetite and began to clear away the empty containers. I stood at the sink with my hands in the soapy dishwater as I thought about what I learned. Grant admitted to dating a married woman, probably Carla. I didn't believe that he was back in town and didn't realize Carla was a married woman. I wanted to call him out on his lie. If he was the murderer, I didn't think that would be the best idea in the world. I imagined the headline, "Librarian Murdered by Moo Shoo Pork Mad Man!"

"Wade brought me a change of clothes. I'm going to shower while he gets my things out of the car. He needs to grab his wheelchair, too. We'll be in the next room if you need us." Juliet headed down the hallway, and I was alone with Grant. They may not think he was a threat, but evidence to the contrary was building.

"You want me to help you wash?" Grant had a clean dishtowel in his hands. He picked up a glass and dried it.

"That's okay. I can do it. You must be tired after working all day. You can head on home. Wade and Juliet promised to hang around tonight. I should get some sleep after last night. I'm exhausted."

"I wish I had been here for you, Phee." His voice softened and he said, "I know we're just friends, but I'm here for you if you need me. One day if you decide you want to be more than just friends…"

"Grant, I don't think I will see you in any other light than as a friend. I'm sorry." I didn't meet his eyes. I walked a thin line here, but I needed him to know that I saw him as a friend, not a lover. "I wasn't going to say anything, but I guess I should. I'm seeing Clint." I said it quickly and waited for his reaction. My hands gripped a fork under the bubbles in case I had to defend myself.

"That's great, Phee," Grant said. I looked up at him with surprise. "What? Listen, I'll admit I have feelings for you, but you've been my best friend for years. I want you to be happy. If Clint makes you happy, then I'm glad. A little hurt and a whole lot jealous, but I tried. I guess it wasn't meant to be. I'll be here to pick up the pieces if it doesn't work out though. I know you've been half in love with Clint for years, but his track record with women isn't the best. From what I hear, he changes women as often as I change my underwear."

I felt the tension slide away and I released the fork. He wasn't the killer. Snotty comment about Clint aside, he wasn't upset about Clint and me. A killer would have reacted with anger instead of calm acceptance. I stopped worrying I'd die by chopstick. "I know Clint's dated a lot of women, but I've got to take a chance. Thanks for making me feel like crap!" I teased him. "Grant, you're a great guy. We've been through thick and thin together, but you and I have no chemistry. Maybe it's because you shoved a green bean up your nose on a dare when you were fifteen."

"I defended my honor. I rose to the challenge of nose-stuffing at the lunch table and emerged victorious." He thrust out his chest like a knight in shining armor. "I learned a valuable lesson that day. Never pick dare again during a game of Truth or Dare against Phee Jefferson. You play for keeps."

"You really are the best. Some woman will be lucky to have you. Then I'll probably hate her for stealing away my friend." I gave him a fierce hug.

"I'll make sure she is tall and blonde and a cheerleader. Paybacks for the green bean debacle." He play punched me lightly on the arm.

"Speaking of tall, blonde cheerleaders, was the married woman Carla?" I asked. Forget subtle. I needed to know.

"Yeah, it was." Grant refused to meet my gaze. "It was right after I moved back into town and looking for a house. She was my real estate agent. To be honest, she said she was separated, but I knew it was a lie. I let myself believe it. Mentally, I was back in high school and she was the hot cheerleader."

"Oh, Grant. I thought you hated her. I never imagined you would sleep with Carla," I admonished him.

"It happened one time and instead of feeling like a big shot, I felt like a total loser. It's been almost ten years since high school. I still felt like the nerdy guy not allowed to sit at the table with the jocks. A big shot attorney with a sports car, a home and a great career, and sometimes I still feel sixteen. Afterwards, I called it off. I ducked her calls for a week. After that, I didn't hear from her again. The only time I talked to her again was at the breakfast. Mad at me?" He gave me a hang dog look.

"No, I understand. I guess we're growing up. It kind of sucks being an adult."

"Yep." He grinned. "I am much more mature than you though."

"Ha!" I rolled the tea towel and snapped him playfully.

"I rest my case," he laughed. "I'm heading home to let you get some rest. Call me tomorrow?"

"Ok. Thanks for stopping by." I walked him to the door.

"Anytime, Phee. That's what friends are for," Grant wrapped his arm around my shoulder and hugged me to him. He opened the door. Clint was there with his hand raised to knock. It dropped to his side and the look on his face was thunderous. I squirmed uncomfortably under Grant's arm. "Hey there, Clint. I was just leaving. I came over to help watch over Phee. With all this crazy stuff going on in town, you can't be too careful."

"Grant." Clint bit his name off between clenched teeth. "Perfect timing. I need to talk to you about all this so-called crazy stuff. I think my office would be a good place to have that conversation, don't you?"

"Sure, I'm happy to help your investigation. Thanks again for dinner, Phee. Call me if you need me." Grant couldn't resist the last little jibe at Clint. I guess he might never give up entirely. "Okay if I follow you in my car, Deputy?"

"That's fine." Clint bristled with anger. "I'll talk to you later, Phee." He turned and strode off the porch towards his car.

"Okay," I said in a small voice and shut the door. I leaned against the door and heaved a sigh. Clint was obviously livid that Grant was here. It wasn't my fault he had shown up. If he gave me a chance to explain, he would calm down. Clint was wrong about Grant, too. Grant wasn't hiding anything. If he was guilty, would he admit to an affair with Carla? To my knowledge, he didn't have anything against Huey. And if he didn't kill Carla, then he couldn't have killed Duane. I sighed in frustration. Investigating was harder in real life. I needed to get my little gray cells working harder.

CHAPTER TWENTY NINE

The next morning, I woke up early. Wade and Juliet were still asleep. I tiptoed into the kitchen and made some coffee. When I stepped onto the porch to grab the newspaper, I saw Clint's truck parked in my driveway behind Velma. He was asleep in the driver's seat. I pulled my robe tighter around my waist to stave off the morning chill and walked over. His head lay back against the headrest and his mouth open. I rapped my knuckles against the driver's side window. Clint startled awake and looked around wildly until he realized it was me. With a grimace, he opened the truck door to step out.

"So angry with me you decided to sleep outside?" I asked.

"No. By the time I got done at the station it was after midnight. I went home, let Watson out for a bit, but I couldn't sleep. I was worried, so I drove over to check on you. All the lights were out. I didn't want to wake you, but I didn't want to go home, either. You make me crazy, Phee."

"Come on in the house and let me make you a cup of coffee. I take it that you didn't arrest Grant?" I walked back into the house and he trailed behind me. "Wade and Juliet are still asleep."

Clint poured himself a cup of coffee and sat down at the table. "No, I didn't arrest him. He admitted to having an affair with Carla, but says it was a one-night stand not enough to kill her over it. I believed him. He claims he was at work when Duane was killed. A stock clerk at Abe's Market across the street didn't leave work until late. It's his job to mop the floors after they close at nine. He left around 11:30 and said the lights were on at the law firm. He saw the shadow of someone sitting at their desk. Plus, he checked out a "sweet ride" sitting in the parking lot. Grant's "sweet ride" was parked at his office. It's not an airtight alibi, but I don't have enough to hold him."

"I didn't invite him over here. Wade ran into him and told him what happened. Grant invited himself to dinner. I didn't know what to do," I explained. "He wants to be more than friends, but I made it clear I wasn't interested."

"I know," Clint sighed. "He was forthright and a little arrogant about how I wasn't good enough for you. He let me know in no uncertain terms that he planned on biding his time. He informed me would wait until I get bored and swoop in and comfort you. I wanted to throw his ass in a cell just for the fun of it."

"Are you going to get bored with me?" I asked in a small, quiet voice. I held my breath waiting for his response.

"Phee, I can't promise anything right now. I don't have a crystal ball, and I can't predict the future. What I do know," he reached over and grabbed my hand, "is that I want you and I care for you. I don't plan on leaving. How about we take it one day at a time and see how it goes?"

"That works for me," I said letting out the breath I

was holding. "I like one day at a time."

"Good. Glad that's settled because I'd hate to punch Grant in his perfect little teeth," Clint deadpanned.

"Clint! That's not funny. Grant was my friend when I had braces and Christmas tree-shaped hair. He's a good guy. You'd like him if you got to know him," I said.

"I'll take your word for it," Clint grimaced. "I'm at a standstill with this investigation now that Grant is cleared. Maybe I've got it all wrong, and it isn't related to you. The rose could be a random prank. I keep picking away at the threads connecting all the cases and coming up empty. There has to be something that ties them together."

"I hope you figure it out before someone else gets killed." I wondered who would be next. "I'd better get ready for work. It's only me until this afternoon, so I need to shower."

"Do you need some help?" Clint did a lascivious raising of his brows. "I'm here to be your bodyguard. I shouldn't leave you alone in the shower."

I got up and held out my hand to him. "Let's see how well you actually guard my body." He stood up and followed me. I might be late for work after all.

CHAPTER THIRTY

Still smiling, I unlocked the doors and switched on the lights at work. I put my bag and jacket in my office and pushed a cart towards the overnight book drop. A pile of books were in the drop and something white stuck to the bottom. I reached and tugged it free. It was an envelope with my name. Someone must have a fine and stuck an envelope with money into the book drop. I pulled out a folded piece of paper. Written in block letters, "I TRIED TO PROTECT YOU BUT YOU CHOSE WRONG AND NOW YOU MUST PAY." I dropped it and backed away. I dashed across the library and called the sheriff.

"Miller's Cove Sheriff's Department. How can I help you," a nasal voice answered.

"It's Ophelia Jefferson over at the library. I received a threatening note. Can you send someone over right away?" I gasped into the phone while fighting the my rising panic. I was locked inside the building and safe for now, but someone wanted me out of the picture. They poisoned Carla in broad daylight in a crowd. I wasn't safe anywhere.

"Hold on," the tinny voice said. I heard a muffled conversation in the background. "Miss Jefferson, Sheriff Dawes said he'll be there in less than three minutes. He said to tell you don't open the doors to the public and stay put for now."

"I'll wait by the door. Thank you." I hung up and

watched through the windows as I saw Sheriff Dawes leave his office and stride down the street towards the library. A moment later, I opened the door for him. Charlie waited outside. "Charlie, we'll be a few minutes late opening today. Can you stay by the entrance and let people know it will be a few more minutes?"

"Sure thing. Is everything okay?" Charlie asked.

"Everything's fine. I need to speak to the Sheriff for a few minutes, and then I'll open," I reassured him. I closed the door and locked it again.

"Where's this note?" Jaime demanded. "I swear this town is going crazy. Three murders in less than two weeks and now threats against you. I'm at my wit's end. If we don't crack the case soon, I'll need to call in the state police to help."

"I'm scared, Jaime." I wrapped my arms around me and shivered from fear. I showed him the dropped note on the floor. The sheriff pulled a handkerchief from his pocket and picked it up carefully by the corner.

"Dag nab it! I rushed here without my evidence kit. Do you have a clean bag I can put this in?" I walked to the supply closet and pulled out a large plastic bag we used to hold children's craft project pieces. He placed the note and the envelope into the plastic bag and sealed it shut.

"I doubt there are fingerprints on it. Whoever is behind this is careful not to leave behind evidence." Jaime shook his head in frustration. "Listen, Phee. We got results back from the rose left on your door. It was human blood. Once we get full results back, I'm sure it will match Duane's. The person committing these murders is mentally disturbed. You need to be careful. I don't have enough men to protect you full time, but you should be safe inside the library."

"I plan to stay right here and never be alone with anyone. Jaime, this situation has me terrified of people I've known my whole life. I wonder if they might be a killer or wonder what I've done to make someone angry with me." I shivered again.

"It says you chose wrong. Any idea what they mean?" Jaime asked.

"I don't know. I'm trying to recall if I've made any choices about the library or..." I stopped. "I chose Clint over Grant. It's the only recent choice I've made. I don't understand why someone would want to kill me over Clint. Grant was okay with my decision, so it's not him. Could it be a woman in Clint's life who's angry that we're dating? They could only know about us if they've been watching me. The only people aware of our relationship are Wade, Juliet, and Grant."

"You might be on to something there. Clint's left a quite a few women in his wake. I met a couple of them and some weren't wrapped too tight. Are you sure dating Clint is a good idea?" Jaime said with a paternal tone. "Don't get me wrong, Phee. I like Clint and he's a good officer, but his reputation is to love them and leave them. As a good friend of your dad's, I feel obligated to give you a friendly warning."

"I appreciate it, but I'm a grown woman. I can look out for myself in the romance department."

"Ah, Phee. Don't be angry with me. I forget you aren't a little girl anymore. Just be careful. I'll take the note back to the office and process it. If you remember anything else, call me. I'm going to catch the creep doing this and lock him up." Jaime gave me a reassuring pat on the shoulder and left. I followed behind him and opened the doors to the public. A few more folks stood with Charlie waiting. There was a flurry of whispers as they watched the sheriff leave the building.

"Are you okay, Phee?" Francis Palfrey asked with concern. "What was the sheriff doing here? Did someone break in?"

"I'm fine and no, nothing was stolen. Just a bit of a scare, but it turned out to be nothing," I reassured her. "I'm a little on edge with all of these murders." I hurried away so she wouldn't see the lies that must be written in bold ink on my face.

I kept busy so I wouldn't dwell on the threat that I would be made to pay. As I shelved books in the 500 section of nonfiction, a book caught my eye. *Poisonous Mushrooms of North America* said the title on the spine. I pulled it from the shelf and flipped through it. When I came to the page on the *Amanita bisporigera* also known as the Destroying Angel Mushroom, I noticed the page turned down at the corner. I wondered if the killer used the book to figure out how to kill Carla.

I hurried to my desk and called Sheriff Dawes. The receptionist connected me straight through to him.

"Sheriff, I figured out how the murderer learned about the mushroom that killed Carla. There's a book at the library describing poisonous mushrooms. I remember it was on display when Duane gave his talk the other day. I flipped through it a minute ago and saw that someone turned down the page on the exact mushroom that killed Carla. I was careful when I handled it. Do you want to come get it and dust it for prints?" I placed the book on my desk to make sure I didn't smudge possible evidence.

"It'll be hard to use prints from a book to prove a suspect killed Carla. Anyone could touch it on the shelves, and it's a public library. Go ahead and put it in a bag. I'll send someone and see if we can get any usable prints." Jaime instructed before disconnecting the call.

I put the book in a bag and slipped into my desk drawer. They might not prove the person who handled this book was the murderer, but I guarantee you it would steer them in the right direction. Shutting my desk drawer, I tried to put it out of my mind and focus on work.

CHAPTER THIRTY ONE

I cataloged the new books that came in the previous day. In between cataloging, I checked books in and out and chatted with my regulars. A couple of older ladies were voracious readers. They stopped in every week to grab the latest novels by their favorite authors. I didn't even need to call and ask if they wanted certain books. I just set them aside for the next time they came in. I loved the delight on their wrinkled little faces when they checked out a new book to take home and enjoy.

That afternoon, Wade came in for his regular shift. I told him happened and said the sheriff would stop by later to pick up the book as possible evidence. "I don't like this one bit," Wade said. "It has to be someone who knows about your love life. Clint is the only new thing in your life. What else have you done recently to make someone angry? Nothing I know of. Don't take this wrong, but you're a fairly innocuous person."

"No offense taken. I wish whoever was sending me threats thought I was harmless." I tried to shrug it off and act unconcerned, but Wade could see my stress.

"Well, it's easy enough to see who checked out the book last," Wade went over to the library computer. He tapped a few keys, and he pulled up the catalog record for the book on mushrooms. "It says the last person to check it out was Shari Davis. That's Grant's mom, isn't it?"

"It is. She checked it out the day of the talk. Her

house is right by the woods and she said she wanted to learn which mushrooms were safe to eat since there were so many sprouting behind her home. Whoever killed Carla was probably smart enough not to check it out. They could flip through it while standing in the stacks," I said in frustration. Hopefully, the sheriff would find something to point them in the right direction.

"Why don't you take a break and get something to eat," Wade suggested. "It's slow right now. I can handle it."

"I'll take you up on that offer," I grabbed my purse and jacket and pulled out the bag with the book. "The sheriff's office is on my way, so I can drop the book off on my way. Do you want me to bring you back anything to eat?"

"I could do with a Reuben with an extra dill pickle on the side. Thanks." Wade turned to help a young boy find the latest in a popular superhero series.

At the sheriff's office, I gave the bag to the gum-smacking receptionist. I told her that Sheriff Dawes was expecting it. I hoped she heard me since her eyes never left the screen of her cell phone. Her longer fingernails clicked over the small screen as she texted and said, "Uh huh."

I strolled down the street enjoying the smell of fall in the air. A slight breeze stirred the leaves at my feet as I headed towards Odd Couple's to grab a sandwich. As I crossed the street, I changed my mind and headed towards Maybe Baby Boutique. I thought about the possibility that whoever targeting me did it because of my tie to Clint. The only person fitting that description was Valerie Hill.

The chime rang out *Brahms's Lullaby* and Valerie glanced up from a table where she straightened baby blankets. "Hi, Phee. Are you here to buy something else for the twins?" Valerie looked striking with her dark hair contrasting with the light pink sweater that clung to her curvaceous figure.

"I wanted to pick up a few more things before the baby shower. Some blankets would be nice since it will be cold when they come home from the hospital in November. I guess coming back to Miller's Cove is a big change after living in New York City."

"It's a little hard to adjust, but I'm glad to be back," Valerie admitted. She straightened a stack of blue blankets. She held a gorgeous blue and yellow one up to show me. "This would be great for your nephew."

"It's perfect," I admitted. "Do you have a complementary one for my niece?" I pretended to browse through the baby clothes. "Have you been seeing anyone since you moved back or have you been too busy getting the store opened?" I tried to sound casual, but inside my stomach knotted. If Valerie was guilty, I didn't want her to know what I suspected.

"I've been busy opening the boutique. Plus, my son runs me ragged." Valerie found a pink and yellow blanket and held it out.

"You have a son? How old is he?"

"He's three and a handful." Valerie reached around the counter and handed me a picture frame. It contained a photograph of a toddler with curly brown hair and bright blue eyes. "His name is Jacob."

"He's adorable," I smiled at her. "You must be one proud mom. It has to be tough raising a son on your own." I doubted Valerie could be out and about killing people if she had a young son with her.

"Well, I hope I won't be raising him on my own," Valerie wrapped the blankets up for me.

"Really?" My senses went on high alert. I might be on to something. I might get her to slip up and confess.

"Yeah. My ex and I've been talking since I moved back. He's discovered life as a single guy isn't what he expected it to be. We've talked, and he's thinking of opening up a small firm in Burlington. He's planning a trip here next weekend to view potential offices. I'm crossing my fingers." Valerie held up her two crossed fingers and smiled at me. She wasn't the mean girl I always believed her to be. I guess life isn't perfect for the beautiful people of the world either. I handed her my credit card, and she rang up my purchase. Wishing her good luck, I stepped outside and headed to Odd Couple's.

CHAPTER THIRTY TWO

I walked in and took a seat at the lunch counter. Debating between the Lucille Ball Grilled Cheese and the James Dean Burger, I heard a familiar laugh ring out above the hubbub of diners. Turning my stool so I could survey the restaurant, I spotted Mom and Juliet at a corner booth. I worked my way through the crowded diner. Mom looked up and smiled, "Why hello, sweetheart! Have you eaten yet? Come join us!"

I sat down next to Juliet and when she didn't scooch over, I pinched her arm. "Ouch! Mom, Phee's pinching me!" Juliet tattled.

"I don't know what she's talking about?" I gave Juliet an innocent look and stuck out my tongue at her.

"You girls behave! I swear it's like you are both twelve years old. What are you doing today, Phee? Are you off work?" Mom asked as she glanced over the menu. "I think I'll have the Judy Garland Cobb Salad and water with lemon."

"Nothing much. Just trying to figure out who's bumping off the people of Miller's Cove," I said casually. I unwrapped my silverware from the paper napkin and placed it on my lap. Juliet opened her mouth and closed it. She resembled a beached fish gasping for air. She kicked me in the ankle. Her expression said I was crazy.

"That's nice, dear. Make sure you're careful," Mom continued to look at the menu. Juliet and I sat with our mouths gaped in surprise. I hope no fisherman were nearby because now we both looked like beached fish. I mouthed to Juliet asking her if mom had lost her mind. Juliet shook her head and shrugged.

"Mom, did you hear what I said? I said I'm trying to solve a murder," I repeated to her in a louder voice. I should take her to get her hearing check. She was still young, but you never know.

"I heard what you said. I am neither deaf nor crazy. You're an intelligent girl and if you are using your brain to solve a crime then I'm proud of you. Just make sure you're sticking to armchair sleuthing and leave the real investigation to Jaime and Clint," Mom warned.

"You know me, Mom. I prefer my mysteries leather bound and two hundred pages." I kicked Juliet under the table. I felt the daggers from her without even turning my head.

"Are you ladies ready to order?" Seth Hansen asked with pencil poised.

"Are you on waitress duty today?" Juliet teased. "I'll take the Lucille Ball with a side of fries and a cherry cola, please."

"Stephanie is stuck on the phone with one of our vendors trying to straighten out an order. I make a kick butt waitress, thank you very much!" Seth joked. "How about you, Phee. What would you like?"

"The same as Juliet, please, but make mine a root beer instead of cherry cola." I handed him my menu.

"I'm watching my girlish figure. The Judy Garland with the dressing on the side and water with lemon, please." Mom handed Seth her menu and slid out of her seat. "I'm going to step over and say hi to Reverend and Mrs. Taylor. The potluck at the church is tonight and I want to see what they suggest I bring. I'll be right back, girls."

As soon as Mom left, I told Juliet about the note and the book I discovered in the library. "I talked to Valerie Hill, too. At first I thought she was still carrying a torch for Clint, but she's trying to get back with her ex-husband. I'll show you the blankets I bought for the twins later. I don't want to risk getting food on them, but trust me when I say that Carrie will love them."

"When is Sheriff Dawes going to let you know if he could get prints off the note or the book? You are a little too calm for someone who has received a death threat," Juliet commented. "I think I would be a hot mess and hiding in my closet until the cops caught the perpetrator. Did you like how I just used a cop word? Perpetrator. Perp."

"Yeah, yeah. You are the next Pepper Anderson." I took a sip of the root beer that Seth placed in front of me. "Sheriff Dawes didn't say when he might have prints, but he didn't feel confident that the perp would have left any behind. I'm calm because when you think about it, no one else received warnings that we know of. Whoever committed these murders seems like they are trying to warn me off rather than hurt me. Plus, if I don't act calm, I'll turn into a screaming, crying, snotty mess and nobody wants to deal with that drama."

"I don't know who this Pepper Anderson character is, but her name is B.A. Change of subject. Here comes Mom." Juliet's voice lowered to a whisper, "Do not let

Mom and Dad know that we are interrogating people. They would freak."

"No duh. So, Mom, how are the Taylors?" I asked my mother as she slid back into her seat. "What time is the potluck dinner service this evening?" Reverend Taylor was the pastor at the Miller's Cove Community Church a few blocks down from my house on Willow Street. Reverend Taylor had also attended Duane's nature talk at the library. I just might need to have a talk with him this evening.

"They're both doing well. They are looking forward to their daughter coming home from college during her Thanksgiving break. The potluck starts at six o'clock and the service begins about a half an hour after that once everyone gets their plates filled. I'll bring my famous brownies with cream cheese frosting." Mom took a bite of her salad. She nibbled at her food like a little rabbit. I wouldn't be surprised if her nose wiggled while she ate one day. "That reminds me, I need to remember to call Shari. Reverend Taylor wanted to invite her this evening, but she doesn't answer her phone. Have you talked to Grant today?"

"No. I haven't talked to him since last night. If I do, I will tell him about the potluck," I said.

"What's going on with you two? Last time I talked to Shari, she was pretty insistent that you and Grant were together. I told her I didn't think you were seeing anyone, but she insisted that you were dating hot and heavy," Mom said.

"Grant and I are just friends, and it is all we will ever be. I feel like a broken record. Everyone thinks we're dating and I keep letting them know, we're not. It must be wishful thinking on Shari's part. Anyway, Juliet and I thought that we should go to the service this evening," I said. Juliet glared at me. Her look said that I had sprouted a second head when she wasn't looking.

"Oh, that would be wonderful! Your father will be thrilled. I'll even make an extra dish for you two girls to bring since I know you won't have time to fix one yourselves with your busy schedules." She gave us both a pleased smile. I usually went to church on Sundays with my parents, but Juliet stopped going once she started exploring chakras, Zen Buddhism and shamanism. Mom also knew Juliet didn't cook. She could barely boil water.

"Juliet can pick me up a little before six, and we will meet you and Dad there." I planned on spending a few minutes before the service doing a little inquiry into Reverend Taylor's interest in mushrooms. Maybe he felt fire and brimstone were needed for some of our more difficult townspeople. Time to do a little investigation of a possible perp.

CHAPTER THIRTY THREE

I took Wade the Dagwood-n-Daisy Reuben he asked for and spent the rest of the afternoon paying bills and writing book reviews for the Sunday edition of the paper. I had a weekly column where I wrote about new books, programs and ideas to encourage children to read. Some weeks the words just wrote themselves. Other days, like today, I struggled to get even two paragraphs written. Finally, it was five o'clock and time to go home. Wade and I closed everything together, and he walked me to Velma. It made me happy every time I saw him walk. I told him good night and drove home to get ready for church.

Ferdie ate his kibbles while I fixed myself a cup of peppermint tea. I took my mug into my bedroom and looked through my closet to find appropriate attire for the evening's events. I needed something that said demure and wholesome, yet gave off a clear Nancy Drew vibe so I could channel her investigative skills. I found a sapphire blue vintage suit and a pair of black Mary Jane pumps. Perfect. I added a pair of small sapphire stud earrings and a spritz of Chanel perfume.

At fifteen minutes before six, Juliet honked her horn. Once I settled into the passenger seat, she read me the riot act. "I don't do organized religion. I can't believe you volunteered me to come with you. You will owe me for the next year!"

"I needed your help to investigate Reverend Taylor.

He went to Duane's talk on mushrooms, and he attended the benefit breakfast. He gives the opening prayer every year. I need to find out if and how he is tied to Huey Long," I explained to her.

Slightly mollified, Juliet said, "Huey was the devil and Reverend Taylor was trying to exorcise his demons." She laughed at her own joke. I rolled my eyes.

"You should go on the road with that comedy act, Juls. Listen, I need you to talk to Mrs. Taylor and find out where the Reverend was the night of Huey's death. While you do that, I will ask Reverend Taylor about mushrooms." Juliet pulled into the church's parking lot. Mom and Dad's car was already in the lot, so we went inside to find them. I spotted Dad over by the coffee urn talking to Reverend Taylor. Perfect.

"Good evening, Reverend Taylor. Hey, Dad," I greeted them both. I grabbed a cup and filled it with coffee from the urn.

"How are you, Phee? I planned to talk to you on Sunday about assisting with the children's Christmas play. Since you're here now, what do you say? Can you direct the play this year?" Reverend Taylor asked.

Dad cleared his throat, "I'd better go rescue your mother. She's cornered by Mrs. Grimes. Come find me in a few minutes, Phee, and we'll all get a table together."

"I'd be happy to help you with the play, Reverend. Let me know when I need to start with the kids," I agreed. I loved working with the Sunday school classes on the annual nativity play. The church borrowed a miniature donkey to add to the authenticity. It was exciting to see if JoJo would cooperate. "It was great seeing you the other day at the library. It's so sad about Duane."

"I heard. It's sad, but he's in a better place. I enjoyed talking with that young man. Patricia and I were planning on hiking the Appalachian Trail next year, and Duane was helpful in showing us how to identify edible plants. We'll stick to fiddleheads and ramps. Mushrooms seemed a little too dangerous. He even gave me a great pocket guide to carry in my pack." Reverend Taylor gave a mournful shake of his head. "I'll pray for the troubled soul who is committing these murders. It's just shaken this town to its core."

"Duane and I went to high school together. I'm still in shock over his murder. Clint Mason came by that night and told me about it." I waited. Would Reverend Taylor fall into my oh-so-clever and subtle verbal trap?

"I didn't hear about it until late the next morning. I had spent most of the night at Shady Acres sitting with Mrs. Jasper. She passed away late that evening. I hope I was a comfort to her in her final hours." Reverend Taylor's mournful face resembled a basset hound's.

"I hadn't heard about Mrs. Jasper. Sorry to lose such a wonderful member of the congregation. She used to volunteer at the library when I was a little girl. I'm sure you brought her comfort," I reassured him. "Juliet is trying to grab my attention. It looks like dinner is about to be served, so I'll let you go."

"That's my cue to get ready to say grace. Nice talking to you, Phee. Thanks for volunteering."

Reverend Taylor walked towards the makeshift pulpit we used in the church basement for potlucks. I walked over to Juliet, but before I could tell her what I heard, Reverend Taylor cleared his throat to get everyone's attention.

"Good evening, folks. We are gathered here this evening to join in fellowship and to share in some good grub!" Chuckles sounded around the room. "We give thanks for the food in front of us tonight and give thanks for the opportunity to be together as a church and as a community. Please watch over us as we mourn our recently departed church members Thelma Jasper, Huey Long, Carla Karsen and Duane Phillips. And we ask your forgiveness for the poor soul who has committed the recent crimes here in our small town. Amen."

"Amen," I joined the congregation in ending the prayer. Juliet and I joined the line and filled our plates with ham, baked beans, mashed potatoes and a roll. I hoped I would have room for Mom's famous brownies.

"So it turns out that Reverend Taylor was at Shady Acres the night Duane died," Juliet whispered. "I assume that puts him in the clear. We are back to square one on our investigation."

"I know. He told me he was with Mrs. Jasper almost all that evening. Now we've eliminated him." I sat down next to Mom. "So, Mom, how is Mrs. Grimes?"

"Fine. Still deaf as a post, but her cat, Samson, is recovering from a urinary tract infection. I heard all about it in loud, excruciating detail," Mom said. "I wish she would get a hearing aid, but she likes making people yell to be heard."

"Mind if we join you?" Grant was standing with his mom, Shari. I once again noticed how strained Shari looked. In fact, she looked unkempt. The change in her appearance was particularly shocking since she was neat and polished when I was younger. I thought having Grant back would bring back her joy for life, but it appeared to be having the opposite effect.

"Please do." Dad motioned to the empty seat next to him. "Grant. It's good to see you, son."

"You too, sir," Grant responded as he sat down next to Dad. "Mom wanted to come out tonight when she heard from your wife that the Jefferson clan would be here."

"Glad to have you here tonight, Shari," Dad smiled warmly at her.

"I was happy to get out tonight," Shari nodded her head at him, "and I am thrilled to see Phee."

"I guess I must be chopped liver," Juliet whispered under her breath.

"If the liver fits…" I stifled a giggle and picked up my fork to eat.

CHAPTER THIRTY FOUR

Reverend Taylor began the evening's homily shortly after that, and we all listened in respectful silence. Juliet even listened without falling asleep. After the sermon, I ate one of Mom's brownies and a slice of pecan pie. I leaned back in my seat and groaned. "Juliet, you may have to roll me home. I am stuffed!"

"We'll roll together. I ate coconut cake and Mom's brownies, but it was worth it!" Juliet yawned, "Are you ready to head home? I have a six a.m. yoga class to teach and need to catch some shut eye."

"I should stay and help clean up. You go ahead on home. I'll catch a ride." I stood up to help clear everyone's paper plates.

"I don't know. It's not a good idea for you to be alone. I know it's just a few blocks, but with a killer on the loose, it isn't safe," Juliet warned.

"Grant can give you a ride home, Phee," Shari offered. "Your mom and dad offered me a ride home. You and Grant take your time. He misses spending time with you. I miss you, too. I always imagined one day, you would be a wonderful addition to the family."

"Thanks," I responded uncomfortably. "Movies just weren't the same when he was at law school." I walked over to the large trash can and dumped our plates. When I walked back to our table, everyone was gathering up their jackets preparing to leave.

"Mom, I'll call you tomorrow to finish plans for the baby shower for Carrie. You and dad be careful driving home." I hugged them goodbye. "Shari, I'll stop by and visit you tomorrow evening. I haven't been by to visit you in forever. I feel guilty."

"I'll be waiting. If you're good, I might even make you your favorite root beer float." Shari smiled at me. Her face relaxed as the evening had passed, and she no longer wore the haunted look of earlier.

"Bye, Mom," Grant gave his mom a hug. "I'll call you tomorrow. I have a feeling Phee will have me on dish duty tonight."

"And you should be," I said. I waved goodbye to everyone and went to finish packing up the leftover food in disposable containers. Reverend Taylor would deliver the food to our local shut-ins tomorrow. I prepared the various plates and Grant took the dirty pans and emptied containers into the kitchen to wash. Once I had prepared all the deliveries, I carried them into the church kitchen and placed them in the refrigerator.

"I'm sorry my mom put you on the spot earlier, Phee," Grant apologized. "She's been driving me crazy since I got home about asking you out on a date. She has an idea in her head if you and I are together like when we were teenagers that it will give her back a little of what she had before dad died. To be honest, I'm worried about her."

"She's been looking very...strained I guess is the best way to say it. Almost like she is on edge all the time," I said. "She means well when she brings up you and me dating, but I hope you've set her straight."

"I've tried. She just doesn't want to hear it. She is obsessive about it. I probably made things worse by telling her we went to the movies. I came tonight so I could talk to Reverend Taylor about trying to counsel her. She's just been behaving oddly since Dad died. I was hoping me moving back would help, but she needs more than just me." Grant shook his head sadly.

"I'm sure Reverend Taylor can help her. Grief can do strange things to people." I consoled him. Grabbing a towel, I dried the dishes he placed in the drainer. "I received a threatening letter at the library today."

"What? Why didn't you call me?" Grant asked with a hurt tone. "My office is right down the street. I would have come right over."

"I called the sheriff's office. Jaime came over and took it to dust for prints. It was a strange note." I dried the last dish in the strainer and hung the towel up to dry. "It said I chose wrong and now I must pay. But I'm not sure what I chose wrong. The only thing I can think of is that I am dating Clint now and somebody doesn't like it. I thought it might be Valerie since she and Clint were a hot item back in the day, but it's not."

Grant had a strange expression on his face. "Phee, could it be someone wanted you to choose me and not Clint?"

"Maybe, but everyone in town knows we're buddies, not lovers. I've been racking my brain all day and I just can't figure it out." I sighed. "Well, we're done here. You ready to go?"

"Sure," Grant turned the lights off in the kitchen and we headed out of the church. He locked the basement door behind him, and we went to his car.

"I like this car of yours," I said as I slipped in and gave the leather interior an appreciative sniff. "Don't get me wrong. I love Velma and couldn't drive anything but her; however, I feel sophisticated riding in this car with you. Like Sophia Loren."

"Well if you ever change your mind and decide that I am the guy for you...." Grant trailed off. "Just kidding. Kind of."

"So you're trying to buy my love with a car? What kind of girl do you think I am?" I joked to relieve the tension. Grant pulled up to my house. I got out of the car.

"Wait for me. I want to make sure there is no one hanging around in the bushes and no threats waiting on your doorstep." Grant walked around to the passenger side and helped me out of the low seat. "Let me go first."

"I won't argue," I glanced around fearfully. "Dang it! I hate feeling scared in my own home." The glow of headlights lit up the street and a moment later, Clint's truck pulled up behind Grant's car. He climbed out and gave me a long searching look at the sight of Grant and me.

"Grant offered me a ride home after church this evening. He was doing a little safety check before I went into the house," I explained.

"I guess now you're here, Clint, I can head on home.

Thanks for listening, Phee. I'm sure Mom will like seeing you tomorrow. Just be prepared that she might get a little pushy about us." Grant turned and went down the steps of my porch and headed back to his car.

"You want to tell me what that's all about?" Clint said gruffly. He made a point of pulling me to him and kissing me as Grant pulled out.

"Grant's mom has been acting weird lately. He's worried about her. Plus, she's obsessing over Grant and me dating. He tried to tell her we're still just friends, but his mom tunes it out." I unlocked my door, and we went inside.

"Shari's had a hard time dealing with Ed's death. Even though I don't like him around you, I'm glad he's back in town for her sake," Clint said. He walked into the living room. He sat down on the couch and pulled me onto his lap.

"Reverend Taylor is in the clear." Clint raised his eyebrow at my non sequitur. "He attended Duane's talk, but he was at Shady Acres with Mrs. Jasper. She passed away that night."

"I thought I told you to leave the investigating to me." His tone exasperated. "I don't like you poking around when someone has targeted you."

"I was perfectly safe. Juliet, Mom and Dad were with me, and the entire congregation," I reassured him.

"Well, you need debriefing after this evening's investigation." Clint leered. He pulled me closer to him and kissed me.

"A debriefing is definitely on the agenda for this

evening," I whispered as I reached behind him and turned off the light.

CHAPTER THIRTY FIVE

The next morning, I woke up smiling. Clint had left late the night before since he had an early morning shift and a puppy at home to feed. I puttered around the kitchen fixing myself some toast and eggs and coffee. I even gave Ferdie an extra spoonful of his favorite moist cat food. I wrapped myself in a blanket and settled onto the back porch to watch the early morning sun rise above the trees and listen to the birds. This was my favorite time of the day. The neighborhood was quiet and the world seemed at peace.

My peace was short-lived. The jangling of my telephone in the kitchen shattered the quiet. I got up and hurried inside to answer it. It was seven o'clock in the morning and a little too early for a casual caller. "Hello?" I answered.

"Ms. Jefferson? This is Deputy Thompson. There was an incident at the library in the early morning hours. Can you get down here?"

"What happened?" I asked. Dread settled in the pit of my stomach.

"Well, it sounds worse than it is. Someone tried to set fire to the building last night, but they failed to take into account that this building is primarily stone. Damage is minimal, but I need you to come down," Deputy Thompson said.

"I'll be there in twenty minutes." I hung up the

phone and hurried inside to get dressed. I tugged on a pair of jeans and a sweatshirt and yanked my curls up into a messy ponytail on top of my head. I brushed my teeth and less than five minutes later, I was steering Velma towards the library.

As I neared the library, I could see the fire truck with its lights blazing. The firemen were busy rolling up the water hose. I spotted Deputy Thompson talking to Chief Shaw near the fire truck. I walked over to the two men. "Well, I would say good morning, but I don't think that's the case right now. What's the damage, Chief?" I could see scorch marks around the frame of the broken front window.

"No damage on the inside, aside from the broken glass from that window there. To be honest, the main damage is that it will reek of smoke for the next day or two," Chief Shaw said. "I don't know why anyone would try to burn the library. It's a crying shame."

"They threw some gasoline all around the bottom of the front of the library and set it on fire. They must not have stayed around to watch because it died out shortly after it started because once it burned the bottom trim wood, the fire hit pure New England granite and we all know that won't burn," Deputy Thompson informed me. "The window broke from the heat, but other than that, the building is fine. The arsonist kind of did you a favor. I never liked the ugly wooden trim over the granite. The town added it in the seventies and even back then it was butt ugly."

"Is it safe to go inside? I need to make sure the books are okay," I asked. I felt sick to my stomach. Someone targeted the library because of me. My beloved books were at risk because of me. Tears threatened to well up, but I wiped them away. This was my responsibility, and I needed to make sure that the building and the collection were okay.

"You sure can. You'll have to stay closed for a day or two while the building airs out. The mayor has already contacted a company that specializes in fire damage. They should be here within the hour to set up fans to help air out the building and wipe everything down. Mayor James even called in a glass repair company," Deputy Thompson said. We walked into the building. I was relieved to see no damage. The smell of smoke hung in the air and made it difficult to breathe.

"I'll post signs to let the public know we won't be opening up for the next two days. I need to call Mayor James and touch base with him regarding the damage and let Wade and Claire know they don't need to come to work today. No damaged books is the bright side to this mess." I wanted to cry right then. Tears of relief, anger, and sadness. This was a drastic act by an unbalanced person and I was in their line of fire. I shook my head. "Any idea who might have set it?"

"I'll be honest with you, Phee, unless someone comes in to confess or someone was driving by and spotted something, chances are slim. Arson by strangers is always hard to investigate. We'll do our best and send out an appeal to the public, but I'm not hopeful." Deputy Thompson escorted me back out of the building. A Soot Doctors van was pulling up as we walked down the steps. "I'll let you go touch base with them to get the clean-up started. I'll let you know if I find anything else."

I walked over to the van. The two men were pulling out large fans and buckets from the back. They explained that they would set up fans throughout the building to air it out and used a special cleaner to wipe down the walls and surfaces. They pulled on disposable suits and placed masks on as they prepared to go in. I needed to stay out of the building for at least the next twenty-four hours until the smoke cleared out. The cleaner was strong and the smell could overwhelm for the first several hours. Since there was nothing further I could do, I let Deputy Thompson know that I was heading home to make a few phone calls and would call the sheriff's office later.

I drove Velma home in a daze. My hands were shaking and I felt exhausted. Whoever set the fire was the same person who had sent me the threats. I realized that all my mystery novels had ill-prepared me for the level of malevolence I was facing. I decided right then I wouldn't investigate further and would leave it to the sheriff's office. As my grandma always said, it was better to be safe than sorry.

CHAPTER THIRTY SIX

I spent the rest of the morning making phone calls. I spoke briefly to Mayor James and thanked him for his quick response. I tracked down the head of the Miller's Cove Garden Club and cancelled their weekly meeting and left messages for Claire and Wade. Hanging up after leaving a message for Wade, I sank into the kitchen chair, buried my face in my hands and burst into tears. Now that I had taken care of everything, I knew I could let myself cry.

I sat there sobbing for ten minutes. I had cried more these past two weeks than I had in years. Ferdinand, sensing something wasn't right with his human, jumped up on my lap and purred while kneading his large paws on my thighs. "Ouch! Alright, Ferdie. I get it. There's nothing I can do about any of this stuff, but you still want attention." I petted his leonine head, and he nudged my hand with his nose. Once I had stroked his fur long enough to satisfy his need for affection, he hopped down and with his tail high in the air, pranced off to his favorite sunny spot in the living room.

My kitchen phone trilled. I answered it expecting more bad news. "Phee, are you okay?" Juliet asked. "Wade and I had the early morning yoga class then I drove him to the VA for his physical therapy session. When I passed by the library and saw the damage, I panicked. What happened?"

"Someone tried to burn down the library," I stifled

the urge to cry again. I needed to toughen up. "Luckily, there wasn't much damage. The library filled with smoke and it will take a few days to clear out the smell. I just don't know what to do. I'm the librarian, for heaven's sake! I push books and hang out with my five hundred pound cat. I pay my taxes on time. Put my garbage can out on the right day of the week. I even volunteer at church. I'm like Susie Sunshine and Nancy Drew rolled into one short, curvy package, and somebody still hates me!"

"Whoever did this is troubled or as Wade says, a whack job. You should lay off investigating anything and stay close to home until they catch whoever is behind all of this," Juliet warned.

"I plan on keeping my nose out of all investigating from here on out. I think I'll retire my Super Librarian disguise and stick to my boring old regular librarian self," I declared. "Hey, I promised that I would go visit Grant's mom today. I thought I would swing by there in about an hour. Do you want to meet me at one o'clock at the Quickie Cow for a late lunch? I could use the company and a peach shake would go a long way to calming my nerves."

"Sure. I have a private yoga lesson to give to Mayor James' wife at noon, but I should be there by quarter after one at the latest. I'll see you then. Tell Shari I said hello," Juliet instructed.

"Will do. I'll see you then." I hung up and headed to the shower to clean the stench of smoke out of my hair and skin. I pulled on my favorite jeans and an emerald green ribbed turtleneck with my vintage brown cowboy boots and headed out the door and to Shari's house.

Velma purred to a halt in Shari's driveway. I knocked on Shari's door. Waiting a few minutes, I knocked again but she didn't answer. I heard a noise from the rear of the house, so I headed around back. Shari had a large greenhouse where she grew flowers she sold at the farmer's market on Saturdays. She also did flowers for local weddings. If only I possessed her green thumb. No matter how hard I tried, cacti were the only survivors of my efforts.

I could see Shari working inside of her greenhouse, so I called out to her. "Shari, it's me. Phee."

Shari popped her head out the open door of the greenhouse. "Phee! Come on in. I'm just pruning the roses." She held up a pair of garden shears in her hand. "You can keep me company."

I walked into the greenhouse and the wave of heat hit me as I left the chill of outside. Shari was clipping branches off of her pots of roses. I strolled over, stopping every few feet to inhale the fragrances of the various flowers. "How are you, Shari? I have an unexpected day off work, so I decided to come see you early. You promised me a root beer float!"

"Well, I'm happy as can be that you came to see me. I was feeling a little neglected," Shari joked. She moved to the next pot of roses.

I wandered through the benches admiring the different blooms. "Well, I've been a little busy. Someone tried to burn down the library last night." I stopped as I saw several large rose bushes filled with white blooms. Suddenly, the pieces of the puzzle fell into place. Shari was at Duane's talk about mushrooms.

She had checked out the book. She and Grant had attended the benefit breakfast where Carla was poisoned. Shari was a crack shot with a gun. She'd been acting strangely ever since her husband had passed away. Most important, she was obsessed with Grant and me. I backed out of the greenhouse and make my way to the door. I turned and Shari stood in front of me with a shovel in her hand. The last thing I saw was the shovel coming up to hit me in the head.

CHAPTER THIRTY SEVEN

I awoke to a throbbing headache. I slowly opened my eyes and discovered myself tied to an old chair in Shari's kitchen. I tried to move my hands and feet and found that although I could wiggle my fingers, my wrists bound too tight to try. A sticky wetness dripped across my swollen eye where the shovel must have connected with my head.

"Oh, good. You're awake. Really, Phee, I thought your mother had raised you better than to fall asleep at the dinner table. I was just getting ready to fix you your favorite root beer float," Shari said in an odd sing-song voice.

"Shari, I'm hurt. Can you untie me, please?" I watched her warily through my one good eye. She was humming under her breath and moving around the kitchen at a frenetic pace. "Shari, you need help. I can get you help."

She whipped around, and I saw a large knife in her hand. Her eyes glazed over and I knew that she left reality behind a long time ago. I shrank back and said, "I miss your root beer floats, Shari. That was one of the best things about coming here with Grant when we were kids."

"When you and Grant have kids, I'll fix them root beer floats and my special fried chicken." She took the large knife and cut a sandwich in half and placed it in front of me. "I've been angry with you, Phee, but I'm prepared to forgive and forget. I understand some girls have a wild fling before settling down to marry, but it's time for you to be done with Clint and start your life with Grant."

"Shari, tell me you didn't kill all those people." My head felt like it was ready to explode and my vision was blurring. I had to stay awake if I wanted to stay alive.

"Of course I did, silly girl. Huey was always harassing you, and you're much too nice. You never stood up to him. I took matters into my own hands. You can thank me later for getting rid of him. I just wanted you to be happy, and I could tell that Huey was making you unhappy. Carla needed to die. She seduced my son. A married woman and there she was out catting around with anyone and everyone! She was worse than a tom cat in heat." She opened the freezer and pulled out a tub of ice cream. She scooped out a ball of ice cream and put it into a tall glass.

"What about Duane? He never hurt a soul. He was Grant's friend, too." I attempted to move my hands again to loosen the knots.

"I'm sad about Duane, but he saw me take some of his mushrooms after the lecture. I told him I wanted to compare them to some mushrooms I found out in the woods behind the house. Once they figured out Carla was poisoned with a mushroom, I knew I had to get rid of him. He might have told them about me and I need to be here for you and Grant," she said in a matter-of-fact tone. She opened a bottle of root beer and poured it in the glass. If I was going to get out of this alive, I had to keep her talking.

"I understand," I said soothingly. I tugged at the ropes again. "Shari, my hands are numb and I can't eat with them tied. Can you please untie me?"

"Maybe. I don't quite trust you after you cheated on my Grant with Clint. That's all going to stop now you and Grant are getting married. Do you understand?" Shari sat down at the table across from me and pointed the knife at me. "I worked hard to protect you so you and Grant would be happy. You messed things up when you screwed around with that cop. He's not even from a nice family. He's one step up from a bum on skid row. Grant needs a wife who won't embarrass him and is an asset to his career. You're fortunate to have Grant in your life after what you did. I've forgiven you though. Grant had his slip up with Carla, so you get a free pass with Clint. It's time to put an end to it and be faithful to Grant."

"I will. I'm sorry about Clint. It was a mistake. I was hurt and angry over Carla. You remember how much I disliked her when we were kids. I'm glad you got rid of her. I was so jealous when Carla seduced Grant, I acted like a fool." I prayed she believed my pack of lies. I had to convince Shari that I wanted to be with Grant.

"Well, she's out of the picture now. I think a spring wedding would be lovely, don't you?" Shari gave me a smile that chilled me to my bones. She had become unhinged. I closed my eyes and offered a prayer that someone would come looking for me.

"Um...yes, I think that would be nice. What does Grant think?" I stalled for time.

"Oh, you know he is busy with his new job, I

haven't discussed it with him. I think you and I can handle all the arrangements, don't you?" Shari continued with her delusional plans. "It would thrill me if you could wear the dress I wore at my own wedding to Ed. You know he was my best friend and I've just felt empty since he died. But now you and Grant will start a family, and I can be a grandma and everything will be fine."

"Sure. I think that it would be an honor to wear your dress." I felt my vision darken and knew that I was passing out. As I sank into unconsciousness, I thought I heard a loud crash.

CHAPTER THIRTY EIGHT

I awoke to two green eyes staring at me with concern. They did not belong to Ferdinand, but to Clint. "She's awake," Clint said to someone behind him. Juliet's tear-stained face peered around Clint.

"I thought you were dead!" Juliet sobbed as she pushed Clint out of her way and knelt down next to me. She grabbed my hand and held it tightly to her chest. "Don't ever, ever, ever get stalked and nearly killed by a lunatic again. Understand me?" I tried nodding my head and winced from the pain.

"Where's Shari?" I croaked through parched lips.

"She's in handcuffs sitting in the back of Sheriff Dawes' cruiser right now. Don't talk. An ambulance is on its way." Clint leaned forward and grabbed my other hand. "You gave me quite a scare, Phee. Be glad your sister is as pushy as she is. When you didn't meet her for lunch, she knew something was wrong. She insisted that we look for you. She remembered you said that you would visit Shari before meeting her. I put two and two together and knew that she must be behind the murders. I got here just in time, too. It turns out she put mushrooms on the sandwich sitting in front of you. I'm sure we'll find out they are poisonous."

"Thanks for saving me. I'm really sleepy now. I'm gonna go back to...." I slipped back into darkness.

When I awoke again, I was in a hospital bed. Mom and Dad were asleep in the chairs next to my bed.

When I shifted and tried to sit up, Mom woke up and hurried next to me. "Don't move too fast, honey. Let me help you," Mom said as she helped me sit up and put pillows behind my head. She looked tired and scared.

"Can I have some water?" I croaked. My lips felt cracked and my head was pounding. A bandage covered one eye. Mom poured some water from a bedside pitcher into a cup and lifted it to my lips. I swallowed some and then rested back against the pillows. Dad was awake now, too. His hair was a riot of red tufts all over his head and he was unshaven. "How long have I been out?"

"Almost twenty-four hours," Dad replied. "The doctors don't believe there is any swelling to your brain, but you got a mighty big knock to your noggin, Phee. I always said I had hard-headed kids. You've got about twenty stitches over your left eye where the shovel hit, but it should heal up fine."

"Oh, honey. I was scared. And I am so sorry. I can't believe Shari did this to you. We've been friends for years!" Mom's distress was palpable and I reached over to grab her hand. I squeezed it hard to let her know I was okay.

"Shari's not Shari right now, Mom. I think something broke inside of her when Ed died, and she just snapped. How long do I need to stay in the hospital?" I asked. I never liked hospitals and the sooner I could get out of here the better.

"The doctors said we could take you home tomorrow morning. You are coming home with us, too, young lady, so we can keep a close eye on you. Juliet told us all about how you went out investigating. I don't know what you girls were thinking," Dad said. The stern look on his face said any excuse would fall on deaf ears.

Mom laid a restraining hand on Dad's arm. "Honey, now is not the time. We can talk about that once Phee's up and about. Are you up for some visitors? Juliet, Rick and Clint are pacing a hole through the floor outside the room all night."

"Sure. I look awful though." I reached a hand up and felt the rat's nests in my red hair.

"Based on the look I saw on Clint's face when they brought you in, I don't think he would care if you had two heads and warts. I knew something was going on with you two." Dad smiled at me and then walked over and opened the door to the room. "She's awake. You can come in."

Juliet, Rick and Clint rushed into the room. Juliet flew to the hospital bed and hugged me. "Ouch, Juls. I'm a little injured here, you know." I winced with pain.

"Sorry. I'm just glad you're okay. I was terrified! When we got to Shari's house and saw you tied to the chair with blood all over your face, I...I thought I'd lost my big sister. It was horrible!" Large tears rolled down Juliet's pretty face. Her eyes were puffy and bloodshot from the sleepless night.

"Hey there, Flea. Guess I will have to keep a closer eye on you and Juliet from now on to keep you out of trouble. I can't believe you. First, you break into Huey Long's house, and now I find out you've been investigating crimes with Juliet. Really?" Rick came over and patted me on the arm. "Mom and Dad always thought you were the bright one of our bunch. Ha!"

"Thanks for spilling all the beans, Juliet. Sheesh. I know not to give you any state secrets," I joked.

"Juliet didn't spill the beans. I did." Clint said. "You might as well know that reporters from the local paper and from Burlington have been calling non-stop to get the scoop. Jaime is giving a statement to the press this morning. Shari's in custody and chances are the court will deem her unfit to stand trial. She kept saying we were interrupting her plans for you and Grant's wedding. She's lost complete touch with reality."

"How's Grant?" I asked. "He must be devastated over his mom, but I don't think I can deal with him right now."

"He's holding up. He's already called in some big shot attorney friend of his to represent his mom," Clint said in a tight voice.

"Well, he'll be okay once his nose heals, anyway. Clint punched him and broke it!" Juliet exclaimed.

"Clint! It's not his fault his mom did all of this! What in the world?" I gave him a questioning look.

"He came pulling up in that damn sports car of his when they were loading you into the ambulance. He ran over and wanted to know what was going on with his mom and his Phee. I answered him with my fist. You are no one else's but mine," Clint declared.

"Ahem," Dad cleared his throat. "I need a cup of coffee. Anyone else want to come with me?" He gave an exaggerated motion with his arm to clear everyone out of the room so Clint and I could be alone.

"I'm good," Rick said. He was oblivious to subtle hints. I wondered if he realized his best friend was holding his little sister's hand.

"I need your help to carry the coffee," Dad said and guided him out of the room.

Once the door closed, Clint leaned over and kissed me gently on the lips, taking care not to hurt me. "I must look awful," I said with a self-conscious pat to my rat's nest.

"You are the most beautiful girl in the world. Bad hair, war wounds and all." Clint gave me a smile and kissed my hand. "Phee, I've never felt that kind of fear in my life. I kicked down the door and saw Shari there with a knife. You were slumped over and covered in blood. I have to tell you, I about lost it."

"So I guess you kind of like me?" I teased.

"I definitely want to be the only one who can call you his girl." Clint leaned in and kissed me.

EPILOGUE

I carried the turkey to the table and put it down in the middle. Mom and Juliet carried over the mashed potatoes and gravy, rolls and green beans. Carrie waddled behind them with the cranberry sauce. The table groaned under the weight of all the food Mom prepared.

"Go tell the boys that Thanksgiving dinner is ready. And tell them no football talk either!" Mom instructed me. I walked to the den and smiled when I saw Clint, Rick, Wade and Dad all laid back with their feet up watching the football game.

"Mom said dinner is served and no football during the meal." Clint pulled himself up off the couch and kissed me lightly on the lips.

Shaking his head, Rick said, "I don't think I'm ever gonna get used to this. Clint, you realize I'll break your head if you break my sister's heart, right?" Rick play punched Clint on the arm.

"Yeah...yeah. You accidentally break my nose one time and you think you can take me." Clint laughed. We all walked into the dining room and sat down around the table. Mom lit the candles and Dad asked that we all join hands so he could say grace.

"Heavenly Father, thank you for the food we are about to eat. Thank you for my beautiful family. Watch over Carrie and Rick as they get ready to start their own family. Keep Juliet and Phee out of any more trouble and give Clint the patience to deal with them when they don't. Amen." Dad cleared his throat and gave Juliet and me a meaningful look. "Let's eat."

"That was not funny, Dad!" Juliet protested. "I was an innocent bystander. Phee made me help her!"

"Actually, you were the one who said to live a little and quit being...what was it you said? Too nice. So if you think about it, all of it was your fault." I turned and stuck my tongue out at her.

"Um, everyone..." Carrie said quietly.

"Girls, quit bickering. I'm just glad Phee is okay. I hope Shari can get the help she needs. She was always such a happy, carefree woman. It breaks my heart she did all those awful things." Mom shook her head sadly.

"Hello everyone!" Carrie said louder this time. "I think my water just broke. The babies are coming!"

THE END

ACKNOWLEDGEMENTS

A huge thank you goes to my cheerleader, editor, friend and evil twin, Maricruz, who called me and drove me crazy every time I killed a character. She encouraged me daily and gave great advice through every step of the writing process. Thank you to Ashley Townsend for her amazing cover art. Thank you to my staff and patrons at the library who let me model characters after them. A special thank you to Caroline and the real Nellie Jo. And of course, my thanks and love to my husband, Dennis, who doesn't understand this crazy writing thing that I do, but is always my biggest fan.

ABOUT THE AUTHOR

Amy Lilly can be found trapped in the basement of a library somewhere in southern West Virginia where she toils daily as the director. When she is able to escape, she spends her free time raising goats, chickens, a herd of well-fed cats and two hyperactive Jack Russell Terriers. She is married to her biggest fan, Dennis, and has two sons and two beautiful granddaughters. This is her first novel.